BOUND IN FLAMES

DRACHEN MATES

NEW YORK TIMES and USA TODAY
BESTSELLING AUTHOR

MILLY TAIDEN

Bound in Flames

Copyright © 2016 by Milly Taiden

Published By

Latin Goddess Press

Winter Springs, FL 32708

http://millytaiden.com

Cover by Jacqueline Sweet

Edited by: Tina Winograd

Formatting by AG Formatting

Bound In Flames

Morgan Polley is an empath who helps people. When she meets Tor and his family of dying dragons, she wants to assist them in finding their mates. Except for Tor's. She wants to keep him and make lots of babies with the big sexy man. It's getting hard to remember her objective when her hormones go out of whack around him.

Tor Drachen is one of a handful of dragons left on earth, dying due to their mates being targeted and killed before finding each other. He's been told Morgan Polley will be a mate to one of his kind, but who? He's having a hard time keeping her at bay and the thought of getting her pregnant to start a family is a very tempting idea.

A breed of evil dragons is after Morgan, but Tor promises to protect her to the very end. Even if it turns out that she's one of his brothers' mates. If he can't find a way to cheat fate, he will walk away without his heart.

A note to my readers:

Buckle your seatbelts, my curvy-loving word addicts. I'm about to take you on an epic fucking ride through the coming pages of all-night writing, cake and coffee-induced creativity nobody can match. Plus, I think this story fucking rocks! So sit your ass down, relax and read this shit because I lost sleep for you. I love you, my alpha-male-dirty-talking groupies. Peace!

— For my readers

I love you all!

ONE

Morgan Polley glanced up from the children's files on her desk to see who had walked into her office without knocking. Her glasses sat at the tip of her nose and she pushed them up to the right location before feeling them start to slide down again.

"It would be nice if you picked up the phone when I call," her mother, Lara, snapped at her.

She frowned down at her files and continued making notes. "What do you want, Lara?"

"I'm here to offer you a job," Lara told her. She stood across from Morgan's desk and stared her down, her perfectly made up face not showing

1

any emotion.

"What kind of job?" Morgan asked, suspicion raising her hackles. "You know I'm not even on the radar with your people."

Lara gave a sharp nod. "You're right. You're not. But we are making progress with the Drachen. Those damn dragon shifters really like to make it hard to get a hold of them. I need you to come to our next meeting with one of their leaders."

"Why?" She pulled a non-interested face. "Aren't they almost extinct anyway? Why would I care about some meeting between the government and dragon shifters?"

"Yes, not many Drachen are left. I am trying to find out more about their powers."

Morgan closed the file she'd been reading and took her glasses off. "This is all fascinating," she said, not hiding her sarcasm, "but I still don't see what this has to do with me."

Lara pressed her lips into a thin line. "I want to know more about them, Morgan. In order for that to happen, I need someone to smooth the way."

Morgan jerked to her feet. "You people really think you can play Let's Make a Deal with creatures that have been on this planet longer than we have?"

Lara rolled her eyes. "Stop being so dramatic.

From what one of their people told us, they need mates or they lose their powers and die."

She sat slowly, a frown working her brow and a headache pinching the back of her eyes. "Mates? And how the hell are you going to help them get that?"

"I'm not. I want to know if they just die or if they pose some kind of threat if they don't find their mates." She slapped her hands on Morgan's desk. "You can tell me that. From what we've learned, if their mate mark shows up, they only have one week to find the female that is right for them and mate, or they lose control of their dragon and both mate and dragon die."

Morgan sighed.

Her mother nodded. "Yes. I've been told they die if they don't find their mate. But if they lose control, will they be some kind of danger to humanity."

"And who is it that's telling you all this?" She watched her mother turn away from her.

"None of your business. I just need you to talk to one of them. See what you gather from him."

"You're not really hoping I'll sense something, are you?"

Lara nodded and met her gaze. "Yes, I am. And if you do, I want to know what it is. You've always been able to sense stuff from all these creatures."

"I'm not a lab rat and neither are they!"

Lara glared daggers at her. "I know that. But you're going to do this because you'll be too worried about the dragons not being able to find their mates. I know you, you'll want to help them."

Fuck! She knew her too well. Hearing the story of the Drachen, there was no way Morgan could sit by and not talk to them. See if there was something she could do to help find their mates.

"So what's your goal here, Mother?"

Lara raised her brows. "Simple. I want them to find their mates. The last thing we need is uncontrollable dragon shifters flying around destroying the world."

Morgan shook her head and got back on her feet. "That doesn't sound like you. There's got to be something else."

"That's my only drive, Morgan." Lara pressed her lips into a thin line. "Why can't I have the good of the world in mind?"

"Because it would be a first."

For a second, sadness flashed through Lara's eyes. "There's a first time for everything."

TWO

Tor Drachen hated these meetings. "I don't know how I got stuck being the one doing this shit. Wasn't Jae supposed to be here?"

Ker shrugged. "He said you could handle it." He slapped him on the arm and motioned for him to get out of the car. "You're the oldest out of all of us."

Fucking great. "You know that doesn't mean jack shit. I'm the last person you want talking to these humans. All they want is to get into our business. We shouldn't trust any of them."

"We protect them and we shouldn't trust them?" Ker chuckled. "Do you listen to the words coming out of your mouth?"

"One doesn't have to go with the other," Tor

snapped.

"Just go in there. Talk to the woman Jae has been meeting with. Apparently, she wants to make sure we have any and all backup necessary to fight Sayeh and the Noir Dragons."

Tor frowned. "See, I don't get it. Why would they care what we have? Sayeh and his people haven't embattled the humans yet. So far, all they've done is target our kind."

"She told Jae she wasn't waiting around until humans became Sayeh's new toys."

Tor grumbled and got out of the SUV. The door slammed, metal against metal squeaking. He glanced into the driver's seat. "Don't fucking leave me. I don't want to have to break out of these clothes," he warned Ker. "I'm making this as short as possible."

Ker grinned and nodded, his dimples flashing and humor lighting is hazel eyes. "Yeah, yeah. Go do your thing, bro. I'll be here."

He took a deep breath, let it out slowly, and marched toward the office building where their meeting was set. When Jae told him about the woman who had contacted him with more information than anyone knew about them, he'd been concerned.

Humans didn't know much. The dragons kept such a low profile, it was near impossible for anyone to find them. Yet this woman had. And she worked for the United States government. If that wasn't fucking wonderful.

That shit didn't sit right with him. How much more did she know? And why did she care so much about helping them?

He showed the security guard one of his many IDs and watched the guy scramble all over himself once he saw his name. It was the same for most people who saw his name. Not that he cared. Tor had left the significance of his name behind. It didn't matter, though.

Most Americans knew his last name as one that belonged to royalty. What they didn't know was it was dragon royalty, not human. Tor and the others belonged to the Drachen family. The name alone meant power and wealth, but humans did not know much more than that. Still, it got him quick responses and guards stuttering as they tried to use the phone to let their bosses know he was there.

A different security guard guided him to an elevator. The ride up was slow and the guy next to him didn't say shit. They were soon on the twentieth floor, his patience running very low. He might not survive this meeting.

The entire floor was so quiet, he could hear the security guy thinking. They reached a set of wood doors. After a few knocks, someone opened them and he was gestured in by an older woman.

He glanced around the plain office, looking for others, but realized she was alone.

"I thought the meeting started at eight p.m.," he said; he'd glanced at his cell phone at least three times when they were in the elevator and knew he was on time.

"It does for us, Mr. Drachen. My name is Lara Polley. If you would have a seat, we can chat before the other person joining us shows up."

He gave a sharp nod but stood by the meeting table. There was a file with his name on it. He made a grab for it, fully expecting her to stop him or tell him that wasn't for him. Her soft laugh made him glance up.

"I see Jae was correct. You do like to stir things up."

He frowned, opened the file and glanced at a photograph of a woman. She had long blond hair with a fringe and a pair of black-framed glasses. There was a hint of a smile as if she thought about being serious but couldn't help herself.

"Who is this?"

"That is my daughter, Mr. Drachen," she replied and took a seat across from where he stood. She raised her hand and waved at the chair next to him. "Please, have a seat."

"Please, call me Tor. Jae said you wanted to talk to us about something important, helping us against Sayeh and the Noir Dragons."

She nodded and waited for him to sit. He peeled the chair back, its wheels squeaking on the carpeted floor. "That's right."

He sat and stared at the woman. He didn't get any kind of vibe from her so he wasn't sure what to make of her. "Why?"

She nodded. "Fair question. I want to help you because I know you will help me."

Of course. He should have known no human could do something selflessly. He had yet to meet one in all his existence. And being alive long enough to see a lot of history, he had met a lot of fucking people. Some he didn't care to think about because he knew it wasn't worth his time.

"What is it you need, lady?"

"My daughter," she pointed at the photo on her desk. "Someone is going to try to kill her."

He raised his brows. "They're going to try or they've tried?"

"It hasn't happened yet. Soon," she said, her eyes glazing over and a faraway look taking over her face. "But she won't allow anyone to take care of her, so I need you to protect her."

"Ma'am, I'm not a babysitter."

She smiled. "I know you're not. But Morgan is going to get a Drachen mate mark soon."

Tor sat straighter in the chair. "How do you know? Nobody knows when a mate is chosen. One hasn't been found in many years. Every time there is one, the Noir get to her first."

"Exactly. They will want to kill her. Her mate mark will show up and she needs protection. She won't believe me if I try to explain it to her. She'll assume I'm crazy."

He met her gaze. "Lady, I'm thinking you're pretty crazy myself."

She nodded. "Let me fill you in on what I know, Tor. I had this conversation with Jae and he agrees you need to protect Morgan."

"Tell me what you know and I'll decide for myself," he said, placing his elbows on the table. He shoved his black hair behind his ears.

She gave a slight bow of the head. "Your kind are rare. You have fire powers that I won't get into. There are five of you left, that you are aware of. No females because whenever someone has gotten the mate mark, the Noir and Sayeh get to her and kill her before you can mate. Once your mate marks appear, you need to mate within one week or you both die. If you or she are killed before the mating, you both die."

He narrowed his eyes at her. "So far, so good."

10

"That means the ones left still have a chance at getting a mate. I know Morgan is a Drachen mate."

"Whose?" he growled and stared her down.

"I'm afraid that information wasn't made available to me. I only know what I see."

He frowned. "You're a psychic?"

She shook her head. "I'm what you would call precognitive or prescient."

Now she really had his attention. He'd met someone like that once. Only she'd lied to him, told him she was his mate. That she'd never get a mate mark because she was special. That they would be mated for eternity. He soon found out all she wanted was to use him for whatever wealth she could gain.

"I know all about precognition. What did Jae tell you?" His brother hadn't given much detail into what they were dealing with, only that Tor needed to handle it as the oldest.

"He said to speak with you. That you'd help me." She cleared her throat and wiped a hand over her forehead. "I told my daughter she can help your kind by speaking with you today, but she doesn't know she's a Drachen mate. She feels the calling to help others, especially shifter kind, and will gladly do whatever she can to help your family." She gave him a sad look. "I have not been the best of parents, so she doesn't trust me."

"What am I supposed to tell her then?"

She shoved the folder closer to him. "This is all her information. If you agree to letting her help you, we can find a reason to keep you near her and ensure nothing happens."

He didn't like this. Lies weren't the way to go. "Maybe instead of making up a story, I should meet her first."

She opened her mouth then someone knocked on the door.

THREE

Morgan pushed the strands of blond hair that came loose from her bun behind her ear and smoothed the front of her outfit. She hadn't gone home from the office and now hated that she still wore the damn skirt suit she disliked with a passion.

Her best friend Lexi had told her to stop wearing the damn things. She had her own practice and could wear whatever she wanted, but Morgan liked giving a professional impression to her young clients.

As a child therapist, she handled a lot of cases of children who didn't have anyone they could talk to. She became that person. The one they knew would always listen. The adult. Of course, she didn't believe for a second those suits were comfortable for her big hips and large curves. Nope. Not even a little. Her body wanted sweats and comfy T-shirts, but did she listen? No.

She knocked on her mother's office door and waited for someone to let her in. She'd had an exhausting day and would rather skip the whole meeting thing, but she'd had a dream the previous night about a faceless man fighting to keep her alive. The man had shifted into a massive gray and white dragon. It was scary and fascinating to watch.

Most people would assume she had dreamt of a dragon from her conversation with her mother the previous day, but she knew better. This was something else and she needed to know what.

The door swung open to her mother's stern face. Morgan couldn't remember the last time she'd seen Lara smile. Hell, she couldn't remember the last time she'd made her mother smile.

"Lara," she said, knowing full well her mother had never cared for the term *mom*.

Lara opened the door wide and Morgan walked. She immediately saw him. A massive tree trunk of a man with black hair and a beard that could make any woman whimper. She met his gaze, her belly doing all kinds of flip flops.

"Welcome," Lara said and showed her to the

table. "Morgan, this is Tor Drachen. He's joining us for a few minutes. Tor, this is my daughter, Morgan."

Morgan's gaze jerked to her mother. Lara didn't like letting others know she was her daughter. As far as anyone, including Morgan, was concerned, she had no children.

"Hello," he said in a too deep voice she couldn't help but want to hear again.

"Hi, Mr. Drachen," she smiled, "it's a pleasure."

"Please," he said again with that fuck-me tone, "call me Tor."

"Morgan." She sat to her mother's right, which placed her between the two. "Lara has given me some basic details about your kind." She pulled out a notepad and pen from her giant carry-on. "Frankly, I am surprised you guys are still alive seeing as there are no females."

He nodded and steepled his fingers, an air of authority clung to his shoulders. "We're able to live a long time, waiting patiently for a mate. We are still hopeful our kind will not die out."

Her chest hurt for him and his people. To see the last of their own and wonder what would happen to them must be devastating. "I'm hopeful, too." She glanced at her mother. "Lara told me you can have human mates, but that's as far as we got."

He raised a brow, his gorgeous dark eyes rooting her to the spot. Boy, she felt hot all of a sudden, like the temperature in the room went up fifty degrees. His lips curved up. And wow were his lips attention grabbing. Full even under his beard. Then there were his eyes, dark and commanding.

His deep red and orange aura colors spoke volumes to her. Much more than any words. The deep red said he was grounded with a strong will, power, passionate, and was survival oriented. The orange gave insight into another part of him. Told her he had incredible courage and vitality and was a creative man with stamina.

She didn't need him to speak to know he took protecting his family seriously. Nor did she need him to come closer to know he'd feel warm to the touch and would make goose bumps rise on her skin. He didn't need to say a word and her heart galloped in her chest like a racehorse sprinting for the finish line.

He slipped calloused fingers through his hair, disheveling the strands, giving him a true rolled out of bed look. He didn't fidget. She noticed him glance around the office a few times before finally holding her gaze captive. He spoke with his eyes, and wow. If what she saw was true, it might be hard to give up this man she lusted after to find his mate.

"Our human females have been killed in the past before they got a chance to mate. There are five of us. If we can find mates within the time our mark is present, and get her with child, our kind will live on."

She nodded her understanding. That sucked so badly for them. That they had to be dependent on finding a woman to love and hope they could mate before they died or she got the chance to bear him children. She raised a hand and placed it over his and something really strange happened — warmth filled her chest. It took her a moment to realize they were staring at each other. She pulled the hand back and cleared her throat.

"I'm not sure if my mother told you, but I can sense things." She glanced down at her hands on her lap. "I'd like to help if I can."

"What kind of things can you sense?" He stared deeply into her eyes.

"I'm an empath. I can look at people's energies and know things, and maybe I can be useful to help your people find their mates."

He glanced at Lara. She nodded. "Fine, I can take you to meet the others and we can go from there."

FOUR

Morgan padded up the driveway barefoot. She'd had enough of her heels. Perhaps she should listen to Lexi, but she wanted to give a professional impression at all times. Lexi's car was already in her driveway and she knew her best friend and roommate was eating pizza without her.

She mumbled at her aching feet and made her way into the house. "If you ate all the chicken pizza, I'm going to hurt you."

Lexi came out of the kitchen with a giant pizza box at that moment. "Hey! Great timing." She laughed. Man, she looked comfortable in her pajama bottoms, oversized Pikachu T-shirt and pigtails.

"You look like you've been relaxing." She

dropped her shoes, glasses and bag on a chair and proceeded to fall onto the nearest sofa, lifting her feet to the arm rest and lying back.

"I had the day off from the shelter," Lexi said and placed the pizza box on the coffee table before leaving for the kitchen again. "You don't even know what happened at work yesterday," she yelled.

"What?" Morgan asked, sitting up and wincing at the throbbing in her feet. They felt as if they had their own heartbeat.

Lexi returned with a bottle of red wine and two glasses. "Remember Jennifer Santos?"

Morgan thought back, and their conversation came to the front of her mind. "Yes, the new one that wouldn't say anything against her husband but didn't want to leave?"

"That's the one. Her husband showed up yesterday to 'pick her up,' he said."

Morgan's eyes widened and she took the wine-filled glass from Lexi. "I have a bad feeling about this."

Lexi grinned, showing a dimple on her dark cheek. "I told him he was getting a foot up his ass if he tried to put a hand on Jennifer or her kids." She opened the pizza box, the steam still coming off the pie, filling the room with its delicious scent.

"Did Jennifer actually try to leave with him?"

Morgan knew too many women were under the mental conditioning of the abusers and had a hard time saying no. Even while under safe custody.

"No. I wouldn't let her leave with him." She sighed and sipped her wine. "I told her point blank, if she left, he was probably going to kill her next time." Lexi's shoulders slumped. "That seemed to get her attention."

It would get Morgan's attention for sure. Of course, a man that abusive deserved to be hung by his balls and publicly flogged.

"I'm sorry, Lexi. That sucks." She raised her wine glass for a toast. "To Jennifer choosing safety for herself and her children."

Lexi clinked glasses with her. "At least for another day. I don't know when he will get to her. The kids talk to him and afterwards she is always frantic. I wish she'd stop allowing that, but I guess she feels extra guilty since he's their father."

Morgan nodded. "That's typical. I have a case of a little girl who was physically abused, but still managed to feel bad when asked if her abuser deserved to be punished." She drank more wine. "You know what she told me? That she wasn't hurt all that bad. All the bruises and broken bones had healed and she didn't want her aunt in jail."

Lexi shook her head. "Man, we picked some fucked up jobs."

Morgan laughed. "Oh! I wanted to get home to tell you about my meeting with the Drachen today."

Lexi picked up a slice of pizza and took a bite. She chewed and swallowed before speaking. "Woman, stop waiting and talk."

"I met the one Lara says is the oldest of their group. Tor."

Lexi grinned, the corner of her mouth dotted with sauce. "Tor. He sounds big and sexy."

Morgan rolled her eyes but smiled. "Yeah, okay. He's big and sexy, but this guy is going to get a mate. I can't get my hopes up."

Lexi raised her brows and wiped her mouth. "Are your panties wet? Come on, Morgan! He's probably the most dangerous man you'll ever meet. Imagine all the dirty sexual stuff he can do to you."

"Believe me, I have. Once I was out of Lara's office, all I could do was imagine. I don't even think he'd live up to those daydreams." She snorted.

"But is he single, that's the question."

"Technically, but that's not the point. I'm

supposed to help him and his family find mates. How is it that I'm going to slip into his bed and have my way with him?"

Lexi curled her feet under her on the sofa. "Easy. You say, 'Hey, Tor. I need to lie down, preferably on top of something warm and solid and naked. Are you available?'"

Morgan giggled at the ridiculous idea. "Maybe I'll skip that suggestion. Anyway, I have to help them. I don't know why, but after my dream last night, I know I'm meant to."

Lexi knew about Morgan's extrasensory feelings. She had some of her own.

"Good luck. I'll be happy if I can go another day without seeing Jennifer's husband or you might have to bail my ass out of jail."

"Aren't you dating that cop? What's his name?"

Lexi shook her head and ate more pizza. "His name is Blake, and I'm not dating him. He's just a friend."

"Right. A friend. Like my pocket rocket is just a friend with benefits," she snickered.

Lexi choked on her pizza as she tried to laugh. "You're evil. And I'll have you know, my toys are definitely my friends. What is it guys say? Bros before hos?"

Morgan chuckled. "Yeah, but in our case it's batteries before bros."

Lexi picked up a second slice. "So exactly how are you helping these dragon shifters that almost nobody knows about?"

"I'm going to see if by staying with them a few days, I can sense or see anything. Hell, I'll take a dream, something to give them clues. I'm not able to let this go."

"Your mom did a number on you, and I'm not talking about sending you to boarding school at four years old."

Morgan shrugged. "Yeah, but this is more. I can't not help knowing they need me. Not just anyone. Me."

FIVE

Tor watched the house from his car. Morgan Polley would probably hate his guts if she knew he was watching her home. Too bad. It was part of the job. If she really was a Drachen mate, he couldn't sit by and let Sayeh find her. One of his brothers could lose a chance to have a family.

Maybe even you.

No. Not him. Yes, he found Morgan attractive. Her beautiful sun-kissed skin, sleepy hazel eyes and that smile that warmed his heart had gotten to him. Hell, those lips of hers had made him think of nothing but ways to get her on her knees with his cock in her mouth, which was messed up with her mother in the same room. Not to mention she belonged to one of his brothers.

It was easier to think of her as someone else's

or he'd never get his fucking mind out of the gutter. As it was, all he wanted was to taste her lips and slide his fingers over her face. But he'd been burned badly once. The last thing he needed was to explain to his real mate why he was so bitter about women.

There was no other way. He'd have to watch her unless she was with him. He thought back to earlier that evening. She'd smiled and touched his hand and made him feel…something.

He should focus on the fact she might be for one of the others, but his dragon loved her scent and Tor couldn't get her eyes or her gorgeous pouty lips out of his mind. He wasn't ready to know which of his brothers she might belong to. He wanted to spend more time with her. To listen to her soft voice and touch her. Fuck, how he wanted to feel her skin and know just how soft she really was.

He slid his seat back and readied for a long night. His dragon would stay wide awake while his human side rested. It would alert him of anything happening near Morgan he needed to check out.

He slammed the door to the main house. He was tired, hungry, and needed a shower.

Ker greeted him in the kitchen. "What's up, big bro?"

"Not a damn thing." He went straight for the coffeemaker.

"So, did anything happen with the lovely Ms. Polley?" Ker asked with a waggle of his brows.

"No. Why? And how do you know she's lovely?" He didn't like that he'd felt an instant dislike for his brother thinking of her. Or that his dragon had roused, jealousy alive and well in the fire breather.

"I saw the file photo," Ker said, his silly grin making it harder to get mad at him. "She's got that whole hot schoolteacher look. Reminds me of my high school English teacher. She had the prettiest blue eyes and always made time to explain everything to me."

"You do realize you never went to high school."

Ker tapped his chin. "Or maybe I saw it in a movie. Whatever. The point is Ms. Polley is understated sexy. I like it."

"Keep it in your pants, Romeo. I'm watching her."

"But what if she's my mate, Tor?" Ker asked, his brows rising high. "I think I like the idea."

For fuck's sakes. The last thing he wanted was

Ker having some strange infatuation to the woman he'd have to bring over so they could protect her. Maybe he should do this on his own.

"Forget it, Ker. Until we know who she belongs to, hands off." That went for himself as well. He needed to remember that Morgan was a human and didn't understand mating ways.

"Hey, what's going on in here?" Clacher asked, walking into the kitchen. "I'm out to the shop. You lazy asses doing anything interesting?"

"I'd like to say I'm going to check out how my employees are working on the new builds," Tor grumbled, "but I'm just going to watch Morgan for a few days."

"Heads up," Ker said to Clacher, "I think she's mine."

Clacher raised a mug of coffee to his lips and grinned. "You never know, kid. You never know."

"Listen up, you two. Jae and Drayden are traveling, we'll have to watch Morgan." He didn't like how that sounded. "I'll watch her. But I'll be bringing her here to see if she gets anything she needs to share."

Clacher nodded and headed out the door. "Fine with me. I'm gonna be at the tattoo shop, so just let me know if you need anything or if you need me to take a shift or something."

Tor nodded and waved him away. He turned to Ker. "She's not for you."

Ker grinned. "I don't know why you'd say that. Nobody knows. So it could be me."

The kid laughed and Tor had to calm his dragon before he threw a couple of fire balls at him. Dumbass.

"She needs protection, not some lovesick fool, Ker." He should just ignore him, but Tor's dragon heated up, disliking the thought of Ker flirting with Morgan, much less mating her.

If the kid was her mate, he'd have to get over it, but until then, he'd protect her from him.

"Don't worry, Tor. I know how to be patient. Besides, if she's not, I have a long ass time before I get mine."

Tor thought of Sylvana. He'd been just as young as Ker, full of life and in the belief that he'd get a mate and all would be perfect. Until she'd played him for a fool. Telling him she knew who he'd mate and it was her. Telling him because she was special, there was no mate mark. And he almost fell for it. Until he saw her with Sayeh. Then he'd known it had all been a game. He'd been a pawn and the one with the last laugh had been the dark dragon. At Tor's expense.

SIX

Morgan hated driving at night. Living in a town that was so underpopulated and with so much forest surrounding their mountain, she always felt like she was in the middle of nowhere, alone.

Had her client shown up on time, she wouldn't have had to stay late at work. At least she'd been able to use the wait time to research the Drachen family. Well, what little information there was on the Internet about them.

Owners of many businesses, the family was shrouded in mystery. Few knew they were dragon shifters. Ancient ones at that, but those in the paranormal world recognized each other. Not to mention, his eyes had given a flash of gray when he spoke to her. That didn't happen in random conversation.

A groan left her lips. She wanted to take a nap. It was the second night in a row she'd had a horrible dream where a white and gray dragon came to her rescue. One dream had been worrisome, but two was some scary shit.

Her mind wandered, but she was still nowhere near her house. The faster she tried to go, the slower her car went until her engine stalled altogether. What the hell? She had a half tank of gas. There was no warning light on her dashboard.

She grabbed her cell phone and dialed a local towing company, but they wouldn't be there for at least an hour. She'd be alone in the middle of a dark fucking road without anyone else. Great.

She was sitting in her car when a call came through from Tor.

"Hello?" She wished she didn't sound so excited to talk to him.

"Morgan, where are you?" There was worry in his voice and she grinned. Hot guy was concerned for her, how cute.

"I'm fine. A few miles from my house. My car died so I'm waiting for a tow." Wait a second, why was he calling her? They weren't supposed to meet up for another day. "Is everything okay? You didn't change your mind, did you?"

"No, no. Everything's fine. I was just in the area and wanted to see if you'd like to get some dinner."

Oh. My. God. Was he asking her out? Her heart did the mambo while she couldn't stop the stupid smiling. If her tiny clients saw her, they'd tell her she was acting childish, which was something she'd constantly told them only kids were allowed.

Heck, if Lexi saw her, she'd probably encourage her to get naked and wait for Tor in her birthday suit. To help him move things along, of course. "Um, sure. If you don't mind coming to get me," she glanced around, "somewhere on the main road toward my house."

"Yeah, I can get you, no problem," he replied. "Morgan, be careful."

"I am. I'm just sitting here—" she stopped talking when she saw a giant black shadow heading her way from under the bright moonlight.

"Morgan?" he asked, urgency in his voice.

She gasped when she saw the darkness move. "What the fuck is that?"

"What, Morgan? What are you seeing?" His voice became more forceful.

"I don't know," she mumbled. "I don't see anything but blackness."

31

"Stay in the car. Don't go anywhere."

Really? Like she'd get out to investigate. She wasn't some dumb blonde in a B-rated horror movie. Did she look stupid to him? Her gut screamed to arm herself. She glanced around the inside of her car but all she had was her cell phone and her big ass file bag. Fuck!

Something scraped across the metal top of her car, making a thin screeching sound she winced at. Her ears felt like they'd started bleeding from the high-pitched shriek of something scratching at the metal. Worse than fingernails down a chalkboard.

She yanked off her seatbelt and dove down, searching under the seat for something, anything, to use as a weapon. Her glasses slid off her nose and fell into the damn spot between the seat and the cup holder she could never get to.

She hadn't even worn her heels today or she could have had that at hand. Now all she had was her cell phone and foul language, neither of which would impress whatever was opening her car like a sardines can.

Another swipe on the left side of her seat and she found nothing. A quick scan of the back seat and she saw the metal statue of an angel a client's mother recently gifted her.

She gripped the cold metal with one hand and

the moment massive claws slid through the roof, she bashed them. Adrenaline buzzed through her body, making her hyper aware of everything. Like the fact the claws were still in the roof of her car and it looked like they were going to pull the roof off. She watched the metal bend and whine.

The whole car shook as if the animal were grappling with the roof. She unlocked the door, ready to make a run for it the minute the metal above her came off. No fucking way she'd stay in the car to be turned into a late night snack.

The metal jerked above her, sides peeling away. She held on to the metal figurine and the door handle. The top of the car wrenched away and she scrambled out and ran blindly for the trees. The sound of a massive thump and the ground shaking made her look over her shoulder.

Bright moonlight showed two giant animals roaring. One shot up into the sky. Though it was nighttime, the full moon gave her the ability to continue watching the dark figure as it fought to get away from the other.

They swooped down and she got a clear view of them. One was a black dragon, his eyes bright red. The other was a white and gray dragon. She couldn't make colors out exactly but she knew those wings and those bodies.

The black flung his tail at the white, but the white was faster. He dodged every one of the slams at his wings. She gulped back the stone in her throat. Her emotions were pulled left and right by the white dragon. Oh my god! This was the same dragon from her dreams. The one that saved her. He was there now, doing exactly what she'd dreamt.

The black dragon backed away and blew out a long red line of fire at the white dragon. It looked huge and for a second, her heart stopped but the white one was once again faster and dodged the fire. In turn, the white roared and his scales appeared to change from white to blue before her eyes.

He flew up, then down, avoiding the black's tail. Flying higher, he put distance between them and made a circle. Then he sent a giant plume of fire that followed the black dragon as he tried to dodge it.

The black went higher into the sky and the fire cloud followed him as if having locked onto the enemy via GPS.

The fire slammed the black, sending him on a dive back to earth. She watched in horror as he almost hit the ground before his wings spread feet above the road and shot back into the air.

He didn't get a chance for another attack. The now blue dragon was ready and roared another cloud of fire straight at the black.

The fire cloud, much bigger this second time, zeroed in on the black dragon. It followed him as he tried to shake it. Nothing worked. She covered her mouth with her hands to muffle her scream.

The fire burned a massive hole into the black dragon's side, taking his wing in the process. He hovered over trees in the distance before freefalling back to earth.

She gulped and stood, shaking. Her mind had frozen on the moment she saw that hole in the black dragon. Her stomach clenched like it'd been filled with acid. She doubled over from the pain, falling to her knees. He was dead. She could feel it in the coldness seeping to her bones.

The pain she felt from the black dragon as he passed was too severe to stand. There wasn't a chance to find out about her white dragon, she fell to the ground and let darkness take her.

SEVEN

Tor carried Morgan into his bedroom and laid her on the bed. She looked good there, perfect. Like that was her spot. He ignored his dragon and watched her, but she was out. She'd passed out shortly after he'd killed Sayeh's man.

It was exactly like he'd thought. They'd sent someone to kill her. He didn't know how they knew she was a Drachen mate, but now that it was clear they wanted her dead, he'd never let her out of his sight.

"Hey, Tor," Ker said from the bedroom door; his eyes widened. "Is that her?"

Tor growled, hating that Ker was there at all, but the kid worked on computers so he spent his life in the house. "Yeah."

"If you need me, just call," he said.

Tor was shocked the kid hadn't gone on about her being cute or possibly his mate, but he was too concerned with Morgan and the fact she'd lost consciousness to think about it.

The sound of buzzing from her bag got his attention. He'd taken her belongings when he decided to take her to his home. She'd be safer here. Her cell phone was ringing. Ten missed calls.

He didn't like looking at someone's personal stuff, but he knew she had a roommate. Sure enough, the calls were all from her friend Lexi. While he held it in his hands, it started ringing again.

"Hello?"

"Oh, thank god," she choked. He could hear the tears in her voice. "Who is this?"

"This is Tor. You must be her roommate."

"Yes! Tor. I know about you. She's supposed to see you tomorrow, but that doesn't matter right now." She sniffled. "How do you have her phone? Where is Morgan?"

"She's with me. Her car had problems and I picked her up."

Another loud sniffle. "Is she okay?"

"Yes. I'm keeping her safe," he said, glancing

at the woman on the bed. His dragon was keen on staying near her. She needed his protection.

Lexi gave a sigh. "Okay. Listen, please tell her to call me when she wakes."

"How do you know she's not awake now?" he asked.

"I know a lot of things. Like the fact her being with you is the best place she can be at this moment. Take care of her," Lexi said.

They hung up and he turned the phone off. He didn't want her battery to run out in case she needed to make calls. He knew nothing of her and yet he felt completely at peace watching her. It was unusual and should worry him, but strangely enough, it didn't.

He glanced out the window at the main house. The castle-like structure sat at the edge of a cliff high on the Piedra Mountain. Nobody went up there unless they were in a helicopter. There was a solo road up the mountain and they had enough security to know when someone was coming their way.

He wanted to talk to Morgan and ask about her gift. He'd seen her fall to the ground, a wild scream coming from her. It tore him up to know she'd been in so much pain.

He pulled up a chair and sat by the bed, watching her. It was an hour before her lids fluttered open. She sat up in a rush and rubbed her stomach.

"How do you feel?"

She met his gaze, a world of pain visible in her eyes. He wished he could take it all away. "I've had better days."

"What happened?"

She gulped. "Could I have some water?"

He scented her wariness and immediately got up and marched to the kitchen to get her a glass of water. When he returned, she was still sitting in the same spot, her face pale and her lips pinched.

She gave a soft smile and took the glass, drinking greedily. "Thank you."

"You're welcome. Feel any better?"

She nodded. "I've never felt anything that strong before. It was like the pain the dragon was experiencing was passing through me."

"I saw you fall and I didn't understand what was going on," he asked.

"You were there," she raised her gaze to his. "The white?"

"Yes."

She slipped her tongue over her bottom lip. "How were you able to go from white to blue? I didn't realize your scales could change."

He gave a wide smile. "You paid a lot of attention when it was so dark."

"The moon gave me enough to work with. What happened to my car?"

"I had it towed since it was totaled. My guys will get you a new one."

She frowned. "Your guys?"

"I ordered you a new car. Better than waiting to see if your insurance would believe you were attacked by dragons."

She nodded slowly. "Yeah. That's really nice of you. Did you find my glasses in the car?"

He smiled. "They're in your bag with your cell phone."

She sighed. "Thank you so much. You've been incredibly helpful."

"Whatever you need, just ask."

She grinned. "I still don't understand how your scales changed colors. Can you tell me?"

"The Drachen have unique fire powers, as do their mates after they receive the mark. We are all fire breathers, but the color of our scales will determine the fire type."

She frowned and turned to face him more. "I don't understand. I saw white and then blue."

40

"As a white and gray dragon, I am limited to small puffs of fire. They won't cause enough damage when attacking." She stared at him so intently that he wanted to run a hand over her face and see what her reaction would be. "The more energy needed for the attack, the more likely my dragon's scales change color. Blue allows him to fire clouds of fire that seek and target the enemy."

"Yes!" She nodded and bounced a little. "I saw the fire follow him until it got him both times."

"Right. If the scales are red, the attack is worse and the dragon will shoot out fire balls that divide into smaller balls seeking their target."

She opened her mouth in obvious shock. "But how do they know who the target is?"

"They're mentally controlled by the dragon."

EIGHT

Morgan couldn't believe her ears. She'd seen something nobody else probably had. "Is there another color?"

"There's a third color for the height of a life-threatening attack. If the scales are orange, the dragon will breathe fire blades. They shoot out fast, seek targets, and explode on contact."

"Holy shit. You guys are like war machines."

Had she not seen some of what he said, she would have a hard time believing it. "Who was the black dragon?"

His features turned dark and serious. "He's someone you don't have to worry about anymore."

She had a feeling he didn't really want to

discuss the other guy, but she was curious. She grabbed his hand and held it. "Were you hurt at all?"

His gaze traveled down to their joined hands and stared at them for a second. The heat of his warmth helped calm the trembling she still had inside. He squeezed at her fingers, massaging each and a soothing sensation relaxed the anxiety from before.

"I wasn't. I'm fine." He lifted her hand to his lips. "Don't worry, I'll make sure you're not in danger again."

She blinked the hazy sexual fog away and frowned. "How do you plan on doing that?"

"I will keep you by my side at all times." She had to stop herself from laughing at his words. While she appreciated his help, she couldn't depend on him being her bodyguard. She had things to do and he probably had a life.

"You can't do that, Tor. I have a job."

He glanced at her lips. "You were coming to spend time here in the next few days, right?"

She searched his eyes and sighed. What was she getting into? "Yes."

"Then we will worry about the next few days first. We'll handle the rest as it comes," Tor said.

She made a motion to get up but he pressed her

back into the bed. "Stay. You still look very pale. Do you want something to eat?"

She scrunched her nose. "A sandwich would be good."

He grinned and her belly did that butterfly effect it had perfected. "Anything in particular?"

"Grilled cheese?"

He laughed, the growly sound making her nipples hard. Damn, he even laughed sexy. "I think I can manage grilled cheese. You're very low maintenance."

She nodded. "Yeah. Lexi used to joke that when we went out in college I was cheap and easy because I only drank water. I now drink wine so she says I'm just easy now."

Another bark of laughter from him and she couldn't help smiling herself. His reaction made her heart sing. His overall relaxation passed on to her and she swore she lost the anxiety she'd woken with, thanks to him.

He got up and headed for the door. Before he got there, he turned and tossed her something she would be lost without—her cell phone. She exhaled a sigh and gave him her brightest smile. "Thank you."

"Lexi called. I spoke to her. I knew she'd be concerned. She doesn't expect to hear back from you until tomorrow."

"That's great. Thanks. She'd be so worried if she hadn't heard from me by now," she said and turned the phone on. He walked out and she glanced at her messages. Her mother had sent several text messages asking where she was, what was going on, and finally, was she okay.

The last one did something to Morgan. Her mother didn't send messages asking if she was okay. She replied telling her she was fine and with Tor. That should calm her. She then told her she'd be with him for a few days in case she needed to reach her. Her mother wasn't a warm and cuddly type of person, so for her to ask this many times shocked Morgan. Her mother had built a lot of walls around her heart and emotions, so Morgan never really knew what her mom felt or thought.

She glanced around, her gaze taking in the really large room, and wondered where the hell she was. By the height of the ceiling and the bedroom size, she knew the house was huge. It didn't look like a guest room, though. She picked up the pillow next to her and brought it to her nose.

It smelled just like him. Tor. Her body heated at the idea of being in his bed. Dirty images of them doing things together flicked through her mind. She had to stop right now before her body started doing weird stuff. That's the last embarrassment she needed. She'd heard about shifter's incredible ability to smell the littlest of things.

She put the pillow down quickly when she heard footsteps. A tall man with tattoos and piercings all over stopped at the door. He had green eyes like she'd never seen. His hair was shaved at the sides with a long mohawk-like strip flowing down to his shoulders.

A wide grin curled his lips. She wasn't useless without her glasses, but damn how she'd like to see him clearer. Unlike Tor, he had a dirty bad boy thing going that even came across from his devilish grin. Tor had the quiet, possessive personality that soaked her panties.

"Hi," she waved at the guy at the door. "I'm Morgan."

"Hello, Morgan," he said with a European accent she couldn't place. "I've heard your name all week. I'm Clacher," he said and leaned against the doorframe. "I heard you passed out earlier. How ya feeling?"

"Good, thank you."

He nodded. "Glad you're okay. I've gotta go. I only came to change before I head out, but I wanted to tell you that you're in good hands with Tor. He'll take very good care of protecting ya."

She didn't really want to burden Tor with so much. She was there to help them. Or try, anyway.

"It was nice meeting you," she smiled.

"You, too."

There was little time to think about what he said. Tor returned with two grilled cheese sandwiches and two different glasses on a tray. He placed it on the night table next to her and stood back, his massive body feeling like a warm blanket beckoning her to snuggle.

"I didn't know if you liked your grilled cheese with milk or iced tea, so I brought both."

She nodded and picked up the plate with the sandwiches. "Iced tea is fine, but thanks for the thoughtfulness. I don't actually need two sandwiches, though."

He shrugged. "I wasn't sure how hungry you were and decided you being full was better than you being hungry."

Being near him made her feel so aware of her sexuality at the same time it electrified her hormones. It was so weird. She hadn't felt sexual in too long. Hell, even her mother noticed. But with her ability to feel people's auras and emotions, it was hard to date men. Regular men.

They usually carried around emotional baggage or were detached, which made things awkward. Lexi had tried to get her to go out with some of the guys that volunteered at the shelter, but she'd refused. What was the point? It was like her sexuality had lain dormant.

Her past relationships were always lacking something. She'd dated some nice guys, but none had ever broken down the door to her heart and made her feel like she was in love. Instead, she had allowed her need to figure out what was wrong with her dictate her relationships.

She'd gone through four men that had given her sex, but not once made her heart feel full with love. Nothing. They'd always broken up with her, telling her she didn't know how to open up.

"I can't thank you enough for the food," she smiled. "I'm feeling much better now."

"I didn't realize you could feel emotion so deeply," he told her. She watched him pull a chair up to the bed so close, she could reach out and touch him. She had to mentally chastise herself to keep from doing something stupid like running her fingers over the top of his hand to see if his skin was as soft and warm as she imagined it would be.

"Yes. I'm an empath that's emotionally and physically receptive to humans and fauna."

He scrubbed a hand over his beard. She wanted badly to offer to do it for him. "That means you connect emotionally with people and animals?"

She nodded. "It's why I felt the dragon so deeply. It was almost like his death," she gulped. "Like I was living through it."

A deep line bisected his forehead into an almost fearsome scowl. "Are there other types of empaths?"

"Usually someone will either be an emotional, physical, fauna, geomantic, or claircognizant. It's rare to have more than one ability and even rarer to have the three I have."

He was quiet for a moment and she wondered what he was thinking. "I have a question for you, Morgan."

She smiled. "Yes, Tor?"

"What's the one thing you want most in the world?"

She puckered her brow and considered lying but he'd know. Besides, what was the harm in telling him the truth? "Babies. I've always wanted my own children. It's been hard to admit this to anyone else. My past relationships haven't gone anywhere. I thought at this point in my life I'd have a family, children." She sighed. "God, how I want kids. I love my patients but I want to go home to my own family. To my own babies. I want to bathe them, put them to bed. I want to hold my own kids. Give them love."

He listened intently. She thought she might

have said too much and worried he'd been turned off from asking anything else personal.

She ate in silence and once she was full, she put the plate on the tray. "Can you tell me about your history?"

NINE

Tor wanted to get in his bed and hold Morgan. Until her mate mark appeared, none of their dragons would know who she would mate with, but he didn't give a shit. The longer he saw that vulnerability in her eyes and watched her bottom lip get tortured by her perfectly white teeth, the more impossible it was to ignore his desires. His human desires.

When he met Sylvana, she'd appealed to his desires as well. But she'd tried to mentally lull him with promises of mating and being the one. He knew better. Still, Morgan wasn't just some woman. She'd be one of his brothers' mate.

Her pupils dilated as she stared at him and her gaze dropped to his hands. "Please tell me about your history."

51

Fuck. This shit wasn't getting any easier. He'd never be able to fight his dragon if it was the one who wanted to mate her, but at the moment, all he could think of was tasting her lips, feeling her hands slide down his chest and taking handfuls of her curves while he plowed deeply into her.

It was the human side of him that lusted after her. "Our family's old. There were many families at one point." He never considered if he should tell her the truth of his heritage. Something told him he could trust her and his dragon agreed. "We've been on earth for about sixteen hundred years."

She blinked at him, her eyes widening. "On earth? Where were you before?"

"Our home planet was in another galaxy called Leas One," he said. He saw the pure interest in her eyes. Not the weird skeptical look he dreaded whenever he considered telling anyone their past. "Our planet was dying. There was a dark species of dragons living on the other side of the planet, the Noir. Their side of the world rarely got sunlight, so they lived in darkness."

"Why was the planet dying?" She leaned forward and the scent of lavender filled his lungs.

"Lavender?" he asked before he had a chance to stop himself.

She blushed and went to pull back but he

grabbed her wrist and stopped her. "I don't mean to pry, but our senses are incredibly developed. I've been getting a slight smell of lavender for a while now and I'm trying to decide if it's perfume. I just wondered why lavender."

She smiled tentatively, and the sight made his heart skip a beat. She was so beautiful. Her hazel eyes turned a more golden shade, which he guessed had something to do with her emotions. Like his scales. She'd fit right in with them.

"I find the scent of lavender soothing. Not too much or I get a migraine. But I like to use an oil diffuser at work to help me and my clients stay calm. I also enjoy taking baths with it before bed. What you're smelling is the oil diffuser scent on my clothes probably." She glanced down at her hands and then back at him. "Does that answer your question?"

"Yes," he licked his lips, wanting to pull her onto his lap and find out just how good she tasted. "I think lavender suits you perfectly."

Another wave of heat expanded in his chest. He liked that relaxed almost sleepy smile on her face. He'd let her rest more soon.

"So why was your planet dying?" she asked again.

"We lived in constant war with the Noir. The Drachen side of the planet offered the Noir the ability to share half of our land so they could grow crops and have daylight."

"That sounds really nice of your people."

He shrugged. "It would have been if the Noir didn't want all the land. They refused the deal and instead chose to fight. War ensued for so many years, the planet was devastated."

"I'm sorry," she said softly, placing her warm palm over the top of his hand.

He glanced down at their hands. Hers was so small, so delicate. So perfect. He ignored the burning desire to sit on the bed next to her and take her in his arms. To hold her and make sure she was really okay.

"It's fine. We sent many of our explorer ships out to find a world we could survive in. We were growing desperate." He recalled being a little kid and wondering if he and his family were going to die. He hadn't felt that sick sensation at the pit of his stomach, like acid burning and destroying his insides, for a long time.

"Eventually, we got news that one found a backwater planet. They were intensely behind on technology and laws. But we decided we'd blend in and hide in the background. There were other paranormals on this planet so we wouldn't be alone.

"Other teams felt this planet was too rugged

and primitive but one of our elders swore we'd find mates here. She had more powers than all others. But still a lot of people refused to come. They found another world in a galaxy millions of light years away, as advanced as ours. A large majority went there.

"My parents were leaders of the Drachen. They didn't know what to do, so they gave people a choice. They felt this place would be easier for all of us to adjust to and the promise of mates for their children was too good to ignore. It was most similar to our own home planet. We could have kept searching, but we were out of time."

"So what happened?"

"Our explorer team set things up for those that made it here. We were traveling a really long distance. A lot of people went to the other planet, but a many made it here."

"How did the Noir find you?"

"They stole one of our ships and linked into our tracking system. They were easily able to find us here. It took them a while because they too tried to find a place they could use for their own without having to share it, but eventually they must have run low on supplies. It was a few hundred years later when they'd made it here, too."

"And what is it they've been doing that is

wiping out your family?"

He lifted her hand to his lips and watched her pupils dilate. He loved seeing that. She wanted him, and god, he wanted her, too. His dragon hadn't made a move on her. Sure, he thought her good-looking and liked her scent, but it was his carnal desires that were raging for a taste of her. He tamped down his need and continued his story.

"They decided this planet isn't big enough for all of us. They've found and killed every Drachen mate. Sayeh teamed up with a witch that has been feeding him information every time a female has gotten our mate mark. There were many more of us, but through the centuries, once a mate was killed, the dragon would die."

"That's horrible. So you guys are all that's left?"

"Yes. We're the only hope for our race to survive on this planet. As it is, we never got in contact with the other group again. Some of our elders took our ships to search for them, but they never returned. We are it." He said the words and felt the finality in them.

She leaned forward and stared deeply into his eyes. "I promise to do whatever I can to help. Maybe tomorrow you can show me around so I can see what I pick up."

He nodded. "I can do that. I should let you rest. You've had an exhausting night."

"Thank you for telling me about your past, Tor."

He didn't really want to leave. Fuck! Already he was getting too attached to her. He should know better. He wished Jae were there instead of traveling, but the mere thought of Jae guarding Morgan made him green with jealousy. He needed to control himself or he'd have big problems when the time came to let Morgan go to whoever she ended up mated to.

TEN

Morgan woke slowly. God. She'd had so many sexual dreams. All of them revolved around Tor and her inability to keep her hands off him. Not that he seemed to mind. Her senses told her he wanted her.

That and the way he looked at her were pretty good giveaways. She shouldn't get too close to him, though. She was supposed to help him find a mate. She couldn't imagine helping him meet someone only to tell the future bride she'd slept with the hot as hell dragon.

She was pleasantly surprised to find an extra set of toiletries in his bathroom, along with a pair of sweats and a T-shirt for her to wear. He must have come in while she was sleeping. The idea would normally freak her out, but not this time.

Besides, she'd slept in the giant T-shirt he'd given her the night before. It hit her mid-thigh and looked more like a dress than a tee.

After her shower, she decided to go commando under her sweats and prayed nobody would notice the extra jiggle of her butt. She kept telling herself she'd go home and change, but that didn't stop her from blushing the moment someone knocked on the door.

She rushed over to open it as she put her glasses on. It was Tor. Oh god. He wore a white T-shirt that made his massive arms look like logs. His skin was suntanned and those beautiful tattoos appeared brighter. He was so fucking tall.

"How big are you?"

He glanced at her, his brows slowly rising. It took her a second to realize how that question came across. Fire flamed her face. "I mean," she gulped. "How tall are you?"

He grinned, a wicked glint lighting in his gaze. "Big enough."

Oh boy. That was not the answer she'd been expecting. Now she wondered just how big he truly was. Not a good idea to think about that. Not when she knew he was a shifter and could scent if she got aroused. Lord have mercy, that's the last thing she needed. Especially when she was panty-less. Now she felt all kinds of uncomfortable.

"Is there somewhere I could get some coffee?" she asked, changing the subject quickly.

He gave her a look that said he knew what she was doing and it wasn't working. Too damn bad.

"I'll show you the kitchen. By now, we've all had coffee. Clacher's gone."

She followed him out of the room with her bag in hand. She'd managed to shove her clothes into it. Barely. She hoped her panties didn't pop out at any second from how ready to burst the bag looked.

They went down a long hallway and everything she saw only verified what she already knew. "This is a castle!"

He chuckled, the sound so deep and rusty, it made her nipples pebble. "No. It's just a big house."

"Really? So you've seen many stone walls inside a house before, huh?"

"It's brick, not stone," he said. "And I guess it could be considered a small castle if you take the whole design into consideration. My parents fell in love with Scottish castles."

"I've always wanted to travel the world. After being in boarding school in Switzerland for a long time, I found myself wanting to come back to the states, only to get a job right away and not get that chance to see other parts of Europe."

The kitchen was massive with state-of-the-art appliances. Five people could be cooking and not get in each other's way. "This kitchen is amazing."

"Glad you think so," said someone from the other side of the room.

"Ker," Tor growled.

Ker grinned and came closer. "I've been dying to meet you."

She blinked and stared into his gorgeous blue eyes. "Hi. I'm Morgan."

The guy was obviously younger than Tor and had a fun aura about him. She felt immediately at ease near him.

"Hi, Morgan. It's a pleasure to finally meet you in person. You're much more beautiful than your photo."

She raised her brows. "Photo?"

"Would you like some coffee?" Tor interrupted. "The photo from your file when I visited your mother's office."

"Oh, um, yes, please."

"Are you busy today?" Ker asked. "I'd be happy to show you around the house. I work from home, computer stuff, all very boring."

She had a feeling he was lying to her about his job. Big time. Still, she really liked Ker. He reminded her of Lexi. She took the mug Tor held out for her so she could make a cup of coffee.

"Are you hungry, Morgan?" Ker asked, coming to stand beside her. Tor growled again. "I can make you breakfast. Pancakes?"

Damn. She loved pancakes. But she wanted to go home and get her own clothes on. As nice as Tor was, she was dragging his sweats and she was starting to feel awkward with saggy pant bottoms. "Thanks, but no. Coffee's enough."

"Let's sit at the table; we can chat a while."

Once she had her coffee, she followed Ker, trying hard to keep from smiling at the frown Tor gave the other man.

"So what do you do for a living, Morgan?" Ker asked, lifting his own cup to his lips. The blue eyes brightened and changed into a sapphire color. For a second, she didn't believe his eyes changed color but then she remembered he was a dragon. For all she knew, he could change his eyes to any color he wanted.

"I'm a child therapist. I counsel children who have been through abuse."

Tor gave her a surprised look. "Even though you feel their pain?"

"That's why I do it. There's nothing better than knowing you stopped a child's sadness. I work with children because their pain is deeper, stronger, and can really tear me up."

He was thoughtful after that. Ker continued his chatting about all things and everyone drank coffee. She'd never felt so welcome, aside from her friends.

"We should go," Tor said after they had their coffee. "I've got something I want to show you."

She scrunched her nose. "Can we go by my place first? I want to change and grab a few things since I'll be here for a few days."

At her house, she found a note from Lexi telling her she'd call later, but she knew she was fine. Good thing because Lexi would have been flipping if she hadn't spoken to Tor. Morgan knew she'd go nuts wondering if Lexi was fine had she not spent the night at home.

They were in his SUV when they were intercepted by a big black van. It stopped in front of them in the road. No other cars were around, so it added to her discomfort.

"What the—"

"Relax," he said. "I know these guys. I called

them to take my SUV and your stuff up to the house for us."

They got out of the SUV. She didn't know what to think. Weren't they going back to his castle together?

A big beefy guy got out of the driver's side of the van followed by another guy, his head full of tattoos, from the passenger side. Tattoo guy went around and got in the driver's side.

The big guy came over to them and smiled. She saw nothing in him that worried her, but the other guy had some serious darkness in his life.

"Hey, Tor. I'll take it from here." He turned to her and offered a hand. "Hi, I'm Rusty. I'll take care of your stuff."

She nodded and took his hand. Immediately, the image of his sick wife knocked her to her knees.

"Are you okay?" Rusty asked, his voice high with worry.

She glanced up and met his gaze. God. She needed to help him. His wife was suffering so much. "Where is she?"

Tor helped her to her feet and curled a protective arm around her shoulders. The warmth from his body helped soothe the cold seeping to her bones.

"I'm sorry?"

She shook her head and squeezed his hand. "Your wife. She's very sick. Where is she?"

Rusty glanced at Tor. "You told her?"

Tor shook his head. "It's too complicated to explain. Just know that whatever she knows, she saw the moment she shook your hand."

"I can help her."

Rusty's eyes lit with hope. "You can cure her?"

She let go of his hand and allowed Tor's body heat to calm her nerves. "No, I can't do that. But I can help her handle her pain. I can help her when it's time."

"Thanks, lady, but we're good." Rusty's voice was hoarse with emotion.

She rummaged through her bag and pulled out a business card. "Call me if you change your mind. My cell phone is on there. I'll come. Just tell me when."

Rusty didn't say anything, but she saw how torn he was to ask her more. Instead he took her card, shoved it in his pocket and walked around them to get in the SUV. The sound of tires grinding filled the air as both vehicles took off in a rush.

She turned to face Tor and watched him take his shirt off. "What, um, what are you doing?"

Oh lord. All the muscles. The tattoos. The freaking body on him. She could stare at him all day.

"I'm taking you somewhere. It's faster if we fly." His pants came next. She gasped and he raised his head to meet her gaze. A wicked glint shone in his eyes. The corner of his mouth lifted in a cruelly sexy way that made her want to lick his lips.

"Here," he said, handing her his clothes. She glanced away from his naked form and shoved them in her cross-body bag. There was no way she'd look down. Nope. What he looked like naked down there was of no interest of hers. Liar!

She gulped and couldn't help her vision straying to caress down his body, down to that V from his hips to his cock that made her throat dry. And wow. He was definitely big.

"Ready?"

She blinked and jumped back as if looking at his penis had somehow burned her. "Ah, yeah."

She was too humiliated to look at his face. She knew she'd see that humor in his eyes again. Instead, she focused on his neck and chest. Suddenly his whole body transformed. Muscles turned to giant scales and her eyes widened as the gray and white dragon stood before her. He lowered and motioned with his head.

"Climb on you?"

He did it again so she took it to mean that was what he wanted.

She glanced down at her clothing, happy she was wearing something comfortable but realized as her glasses slid down her nose, they needed to go in her pocket for safekeeping until they arrived wherever they were going.

She finally got on his back, after a couple failed attempts—her legs were short—and held on tightly, her arms wrapped around the dragon's neck. They took off smoothly. She pinched her eyes closed at first. She hadn't told him she got motion sickness. Would it make a difference on a dragon's back?

They flew high in the air, over trees, and higher still. She saw the river. The forest and farms in the outer areas of town. They flew for what felt like hours. She was mesmerized by the view. And the fact she wasn't throwing up. Of course, she had a nice breeze hitting her on the face, so she gave it full credit for keeping her sickness at bay.

They finally landed near a cabin by a river. She slid off and fell on her ass when she couldn't get her balance. He morphed into his human body and her gaze once again strayed to his cock. Holy crap. He was hard.

"The rush of adrenaline makes it hard to

control," he chuckled.

She told herself to stop staring but she couldn't, her eyes were glued to his shaft. Her body heated as she stared at his body. He was beautiful. Every muscle, every limb, a work of art. Then her gaze traveled to his face and she was once again held entranced by him. He marched toward her, his eyes glowing.

"What are you doing?"

Another grin from his delectable face. "I need my clothes."

She blinked and rushed to her bag to give him his outfit. She stood and handed him the clothes then walked off to the cabin entrance. The cabin was a lot bigger than she'd noticed from the air. With her glasses back on, she stared at the cabin in awe.

"What is this place?"

He pushed the front door open and ushered her in. "Liz? Are you here?"

An older woman popped out from nowhere and rushed over to them. "Oh, Tor! So lovely to see you again. And who is this beauty?"

Morgan had a hard time keeping back the snort. The woman was adorable with her compliments.

"I want you to meet Morgan. She's a friend.

Morgan, this is Liz. She's the caretaker here."

Morgan didn't know why, but it hurt her heart a little when he called her his friend. Not like he could call her his girlfriend, but for some reason, she had a second of wishing he'd introduce her as something else. What the hell was wrong with her? She barely knew this guy. So what if her hormones were doing the mambo for him. That meant nothing.

"Nice to meet you, Morgan," Liz said with a bright smile. "Come to the kitchen. I prepared a nice picnic lunch for you two."

"Oh, you didn't have to go through the trouble," Morgan replied.

Liz waved her concern away. "It's fine. When Tor said he was bringing someone, I wanted to make sure my boy and his girl were well taken care of."

Okay then.

Tor laughed and curled an arm around Liz's shoulders. "Thanks. I'm starving."

"What about you, Morgan," Liz asked. "Are you hungry?"

They went into a lovely kitchen a lot bigger than Morgan anticipated with modern appliances in a gorgeous patent red color. "If we're being honest, yes. I'm famished."

"Lovely." Liz stopped at a very country decorated kitchen table with a pitcher filled with daisies and pointed at a massive basket. "You can handle this, Tor."

Morgan's eyes readied to pop out of her head. That thing was huge. He picked it up like it weighed next to nothing. "Yeah. It's great."

"I set up a blanket and drinks by the river. Your favorite spot," she told him. Then she turned to Morgan and winked. "Enjoy your lunch."

Morgan wasn't sure why the wink, but now more than ever, her nerves screamed for her to go with the flow and if he kissed her to let it happen. Now all she had to make sure was that she didn't fling herself at him if he didn't move fast enough.

ELEVEN

Tor loved Morgan's scent. Though his dragon wasn't screaming out for him to mate her, they both enjoyed her company. He wanted her. She was beautiful, kind, and the emotion he saw in her eyes whenever she spoke did more to him than any other woman had in his past. Even Sylvana.

When they reached the biggest tree by the river, his spot, he saw the giant blanket and twin ice buckets. One chilling a bottle of champagne, the other filled with water bottles. Trust Liz to make sure to bring out the vintage. She probably thought Tor had a bigger interest in Morgan than he'd stated. She'd be right. Tor loved Morgan's eyes, her smile, her scent. Hell, he wanted to sit there and stare at her face all day watching the different expressions as she spoke.

He wondered if this was how human men became smitten. He'd often wondered about that. This was the first time he'd truly felt his heart beat for a female. But this was more than lust. He liked being near Morgan. He wanted to protect her. He loved just seeing her smile.

They sat by the river and he proceeded to pull out the plastic tub of pasta salad, cold chicken, rolls, and peeled and cut fruit. There was also a container full of brownies. He hoped Morgan liked chocolate. He loved the stuff.

"Oh my goodness, look at all this food," she gasped. "Do you need my help?"

"No. You sit there. I'll pass you stuff and you can serve yourself."

He gave her the plate and proceeded to open the champagne. "Would you like a glass or would you rather have water?"

She scrunched her nose and it made her so damn cute. He wanted to lean forward and kiss her. She'd worn a different pair of glasses after they'd gone to her house. These were black-rimmed but had some sparkle at the edges. The sexy schoolteacher look was back full force.

"I'll take a glass of the bubbly, because with this view, how could I say no?" She grinned. "But after that I'll stick to water."

He handed her the champagne flute and

watched her lick her lips when their fingers grazed. He heard her heartbeat increase and the scent of her arousal curled around his nose like a delicate perfume he couldn't get enough of.

"So what is this place?" she asked, taking a sip and placing her glass on the small metal base he'd put down so she could slide the flute where it wouldn't tip over.

"This was my parents' home. Well, one of their homes. The castle was a favorite when they were younger, but as my father got sick, this is where they came to…to be alone."

She glanced around and gave him one of those soft looks that made his chest fill with the need to protect her. "What happened? I thought your kind could live forever."

He grinned. "Almost. There are a few things that can kill us. Witchcraft is one of them."

She gasped. "What?"

"Sayeh's mate, the witch, got into the head of someone my father saw a few times. Our medical professional is someone we trust implicitly. But this woman was covering for our doctor while he was traveling. Let's say she did exactly as Sylvana asked. She poisoned my father for days with potions Sylvana had prepared with her magic and he became weaker and weaker."

"I'm so…sorry," she mumbled. "That's

horrible."

"Eventually they came here to wait out his time. One mate does not survive without the other. So it was my mother's last moments with him. We wanted to be with them but respected their wishes."

She nodded. "I can't imagine. Your parents must have loved each other a lot then?"

"They were together for almost two thousand years. I've heard that human couples rarely last more than half a century." He frowned as he stared at her. "I don't understand how any male could let go of the one woman who owns his heart. He should be treasuring her existence."

The corners of her mouth kicked up. "Humans don't have mates. We spend our lives looking for what might be the right person, but sometimes we get it wrong."

He grabbed her hand and brought it to his lips. "How could you be wrong? Do you not feel the intense pull for the person you want?"

She glanced at his mouth. Her scent drove him crazy. He wanted to kiss her. To get her naked and to eat her for lunch. Fuck!

"I, uh, yeah. But emotions are messy. Humans don't have your certainty."

He leaned forward, listening to her heartbeat increase in speed. The perfume of her arousal pulled him in like a moth to a flame. He went closer, closing the distance between them, her hand still in his grasp. He brought it to his chest, then he met her gaze.

"I'm going to kiss you, Morgan. I've never wanted a woman like I do you and I need to know what I'm about to do is okay with you."

She nodded jerkily. "Yes. Very okay."

He lifted a hand up to her face, taking her glasses carefully off her beautiful face and placed them to the side to keep from breaking them. Then he brought his face to hers, lips grazing over each other and then went deeper, further. She tasted of champagne and the brownie she'd been nibbling on instead of the food on display. God. She was delicious. Delightful. Perfect.

The kiss went deeper and his dragon urged him to get closer, to do more. The lust in his veins was shared by the animal. They both wanted her. He'd given up on the idea of a mate, but Morgan, she was something else. She was a woman he could see spending his life with. She was one of his brothers' mates. But what if her mother had been wrong? What if she wasn't a Drachen mate? He could keep her. No need for mate marks. No need for anything else.

If her mother was wrong, if she wasn't one of his brothers' mate, they could have a family. She wouldn't be able to live as long as him because she wouldn't have a mate mark, but he'd be willing to chance it. She could be his. All he had to do was take her.

She ran one hand over his chest, feeling his pecs. The other hand went up to his jaw, raking her nails over his beard. A soft whimper came from her and his cock hardened. He wanted so much more. To hear her outright crying in fucking delight the moment she came.

He would do it. Lara was wrong. Morgan wasn't a Drachen mate, but would be able to help his brothers find their own women. He could keep her. The very idea of making her his, making her pregnant and watching her grow with his baby unleashed a possessiveness he hadn't known was in him.

He curled his hand around her neck, pulling her closer to him. His other hand went to her chest, cupping her full breast. Fucking hell, she was so soft, her nipple small and tight. And she smelled so good. She'd be his. He'd marry her like humans did. She'd have his babies. He'd keep her pregnant, watching her grow big. The image made his balls hurt. He wanted that. Morgan. His offspring. Them as a family. All of it.

Yes, all his.

Morgan pulled back from their kiss, her chest heaving. Her pupils ate up the irises. "Tor. God. You…" she cleared her throat. "That was more than a kiss."

Her voice trembled. The sound said many things to him. Like the fact he could take her then and there, but he wouldn't. He would wait.

"You deserve more than a simple kiss, beautiful."

"Oh god. Tor, I...I don't know if I can do this. You're fucking hot and I'm a mess. Like an emotional mess." She leaned back so he returned to his spot to give her space. "I feel people's pain. This isn't even normal."

"Normal is boring." He caressed her cheek. "You're interesting."

She gave a high-pitched giggle that sounded more nervous than anything. "This is crazy. I suck at relationships. I date these nice guys that get tired of me after a while."

He lifted her curled hand to his lips while holding her gaze. "I don't give a fuck about any other man, Morgan." He brushed a kiss on her knuckles. "The fact that they couldn't appreciate you doesn't make me feel a sliver of sadness for them." He shook his head. "I want you. No arguments."

She couldn't believe what he said. It was surreal. He was shifter royalty. "I'm boring, Tor. I've always been told I am."

"I think you're fascinating," he smiled. "You're

beautiful. You have a kind heart, eyes that speak for you and you're willing to sacrifice for others. And you've got a body I will fuck for days."

TWELVE

Morgan gulped. Holy bananas. "Tor."

"No. Listen to me carefully, beautiful Morgan." He prowled closer, this time he placed a hand to either side of her. She leaned back instinctively, which left him looming above her. "I don't mind my dick hurting and going days without filling your sweet body because you need time." He brought his head down and kissed her nose. "I definitely don't mind you taking your time. When you're ready, you will be mine. You know it. I know it."

"This is madness."

"I know, love. Yesterday at this time, I was trying to talk myself into staying away from you. But my need to be near you, to touch you and smell you, are driving me up a fucking wall."

Jesus H. Christ. What was he saying? He'd been thinking about her all that time? So she hadn't been the only one perving out? Thank god!

"What do you mean? What's changed?" she asked.

"I realized I can't fight this growing need I have for you." He licked his lips and a glow sparked in his eyes. "I don't want to fight it. I want to enjoy it. I want to let it fucking consume me and you in the process. I want what I've been denying myself since the moment I saw you. I want you."

"I don't know what to say," she mumbled, her breaths coming hard into her chest. Him above her gave her some very dirty images she didn't need at that moment. Not when he kept saying so many things about wanting her.

"I want you. I want you naked. I want you spread open and showing me all of you. I want to eat your pussy like there's no tomorrow and I know you're going to taste delicious." He glanced at her lips. "You'll be mine, Morgan. Every single inch of you will have been touched by my lips at some point. Soon. And then, I'm taking your soft, sexy body and fucking away any doubt in your mind about how much I want you.

"Those babies you wanted? I'm going to give them to you. Me. No other fucking man is touching you once you're mine." He cupped her breast and a soft moan escaped her lips. "That's right. I know you love my touch. I will give you everything you want. All the orgasms and babies you want."

Holy Toledo. "A little possessive?"

She still didn't know how to react. He didn't scare her. Heck, his words turned her on even more. She was super slick between her legs.

"More than a little. I don't mind jerking off to the thoughts of sliding between your soft thighs and pounding you into next week. I don't mind knowing you'll be mine." He ran his tongue over the seam of her lips. "But make no mistake, baby. You've been claimed."

Her lungs burned from lack of air. "I…"

He lowered his body on hers, her legs immediately spread to cushion his pelvis. Christ. He was rock hard and pressing at her center. She whimpered and wiggled, loving the feel of him there. His pants and hers were between them, but she swore she felt the heat from his body at her sex.

"We're not arguing this any longer. I want to give you whatever you want, love. Now tell me, what is that?" he asked her.

"Kiss me." The words popped out of her mouth without thinking. She didn't know why, but she wasn't going to question it. His lips came over hers, seducing and branding. His hand slid under her shirt, the flowy material giving way immediately. He was at her bra in a second, tugging at the material and leaving her breast bare.

His warm hand cupped her breast at the same time he rocked his hips into her. Fire raced down her spine and centered at her core. Her clit throbbed. She wiggled under him, hoping he'd do something to help ease her ache.

Their kiss deepened further, his tongue filling her mouth and curling over hers passionately. His hand moved from playing with her nipple to gliding over her belly roll down to her pants. He shoved under the waistband and his hand went into her underwear. She widened further.

Her sucking on his tongue grew bolder, hungrier as he spread her pussy lips and pressed at her clit. A soft groan left the back of her throat. His fingers worked magic, slipping and sliding up and down her slick folds. Two digits fluttered into her sex while his thumb pressed at her pleasure center.

She gripped his hair, raking her nails over the back of his head. Her ass came slightly off the grass, looking for deeper penetration.

A burning need she had never felt before heated her blood. She panted, her breathing harsh, and broke away from their kiss. She gripped his shoulders, biting at his neck and moaning for more.

His fingering of her pussy continued, the slow drawn out thrusts getting shorter, faster, harsher. She breathed in conjunction with each drive. He rained kisses over her jaw and chin. Her mind was floating. All she wanted was the pleasure she knew was coming.

"Yes, baby," he growled. "Fuck, you're sexy. Come. Show me how beautiful you look when you let go," he whispered by her ear.

Her pussy clung to his fingers. He nibbled on her earlobe. She was so close. Her mind shut down. Primitive thoughts of pleasure and desire were all that filled her brain.

"Tor," she moaned in a rush.

"Do it, Morgan. Give it to me. Your body's craving the release, and I want it." He rumbled in that sexy, deep voice that gave her goose bumps. "I am being fucking selfish. I want every one of your orgasms for myself from now on. Starting with this one. Give it to me, sweetheart."

The tension curling at the pit of her belly unraveled so fast, she choked on a breath. Her body shook. Her nails dug into his arms and her pussy gripped at his fingers. Then she was flying. Pleasure unfurled and washed over her like a tide of bliss. She tried to catch her breath but her body sagged. Multiple explosions rocked her to the core.

"Fuck!" he grunted, rocking his hips into her center and sliding his lips over her neck. He sucked and bit. He slipped his hand from her pants and brought it to his lips. She licked at her dry lips and watched his now glowing eyes brighten even more. His fingers went into his mouth, coated in her slick wetness. "I knew you'd be fucking addictive. Now all I ever want to eat is pussy. Your pussy."

She cleared her throat. Spots danced in front of her eyes. He continued rocking into her with his erection. A massive one at that. She opened her mouth to tell him they could keep going, but he sat back on his heels and offered his hands to help her sit up.

"Let's eat. I want to show you the rest of the castle when we get back. I don't want to keep you out too late."

THIRTEEN

Morgan wanted to say they weren't done and that food was the last thing on her mind, but instead she took another glass full of champagne and gulped it. Then she picked up the food he passed her and tried to act like her heart wasn't attempting a prison break from her chest. Or that she was enjoying the food that tasted like nothing.

The rest of the meal was spent with idle chit chat, but she saw the need, the hunger in his eyes. It only heightened her awareness of him. It made her giddy. What in the hell was going on? Had the world turned upside and she didn't know it? She wanted to get back to her room, toss him on the bed. Well, not that she could toss him anywhere, he was three times her size. But a girl could dream.

They got back to the castle late. His SUV and her stuff was there. All her belongings had been placed in his bedroom. She didn't see any of the others but knew she couldn't stay in his room a second night in a row.

"Will you show me to my room?" she asked after she grabbed her bag, ready to follow him out of his bedroom.

A smile curled over his lips. The kind that meant trouble. She saw it in his eyes. "Sure." He took the bag out of her hands and walked out only to stop a few feet from his door and open the one right next to his. "Here we are."

She frowned. The room appeared to be the female version of his. It was massive but a lot more feminine with lilac and gold décor. She noticed a door a few feet from her bedside table. "Is that a connecting door?"

"Yes," he said and placed her bag on the bed. "Do you mind?"

She thought about it for a second. "No."

Another nipple-hardening grin and he was waltzing out of the room. "I have to make a few work calls. Feel free to roam the castle but take your phone in case you get lost. We do have emergency locators on every hallway of every floor. It makes it easier to find people. Meet me in a little while. I'll make us something to eat."

She nodded and watched him leave. She decided to take a shower first. The day's grime and everything they'd done was making her feel all kinds of icky. She stripped out of her clothes, mindful of the connecting door and wondering if he'd walk in on her at any moment. He didn't. She took her shower and once she was wearing a pair of yoga pants and a tank top, she was ready to check out the place.

She meandered through the castle, stopping here and there whenever something caught her eye. There was a set of doors she opened out of curiosity. Another hallway awaited. She walked down the carpeted path, glancing at the giant paintings of landscapes and dragons.

At the end of the hallway, she went through an open door to what looked like an antique room. There were items that should be in a museum. And then she saw it. A painting above the fireplace. She strolled to it, not once taking her eyes off the massive thing.

It was an image of Tor. He was a lot younger from the looks of it, but the sexuality in his eyes and the domineering look he gave whoever was painting him was so damn sexy, she almost wanted to strip the Tor in the image, he was so lifelike.

There were other treasures in different places. She pushed her glasses up her nose and peered around the room. So many items. One she was caught by was a crown of silver with what appeared to be black diamonds on display.

"I see you've been caught by The Witch's Crown."

She turned to face Clacher. "Hi, didn't know you were here."

He grinned, showing off his incredibly handsome dimples. "I'm sorry. I won't be able to stay long. There's a biker group in town and they've all decided they want tattoos. The shop is really busy at this time."

Her brows flew up. "You do tattoos? I didn't realize that. I thought when you said you had a shop, you meant like a store."

He chuckled and shook his head, the buckles of his boots making noise with each step he took coming closer to her.

"No. I have a few tattoo shops. Everyone here has their own business or we'd be bored to death. Plus, our family is old. We've tried everything at least once," he winked.

"So what is this Witch's Crown?" She turned back to the silver and black crown. "Are those diamonds?"

"They are. Black diamonds. The crown commissioned when someone was set to marry the witch," Clacher told her. "Of course, the man didn't realize she was a witch. Not at first. Not until she almost killed him."

She gasped and slapped a hand over her mouth. "But it's so beautiful. The design is so unique."

"Yes. It was meant to be. You can see the dragon breathing fire down on the person who tried to come between him and the woman. The woman is behind the dragon, being protected." Clacher folded his arms over his chest. "The witch was found out when she was caught having an affair with the leader of the Noir."

"Oh my god!" She couldn't imagine what the man in the relationship must have felt. Broken trust had to be the worst thing to deal with. "What happened to the man?"

"He's around. Grumpy. Miserable. Pain in the ass. But alive. Alive and still waiting for his mate."

She glanced up at him. He was staring at her with a pensive look on his face. "Do you mind if I try something?"

He shook his head. "I understand you're here to help us with our mate business, so I'm happy to help however I can."

"Would you mind giving me your hands?" she asked, holding her hands out to him.

He covered her hands with his much larger

ones. His skin was warm. She closed her eyes, going past the man and into his dragon. The animal raised his head in wonder. He wasn't used to someone invading his space. She tried to calm him and tell him she was there to help. He was wary, though. She sensed something about him, something he hid.

Her mind went to a place by a waterfall. The dragon breathing fire down on a bunch of men only to watch as something else happened. She was pulled back from the scene and she took several steps back from how hard the dragon pushed her away.

"Are you okay?" Clacher asked.

She gulped and blinked. "Yes, sorry about that. Didn't realize your dragon was so…"

"Reserved?"

She grinned. "Yes. I'm sorry. I should have left it alone when he got angry for me intruding into your bond."

"It's fine," Clacher said and let go of her. "I leave him to his own unless I need him."

She nodded. "I should get to the kitchen. I believe Tor was going to make dinner soon."

Clacher gave her another long look. Then he smiled. "Ker is usually the one trying new stuff in the kitchen. Either way, it wouldn't hurt to go check. Goodnight, Morgan."

"Goodnight, Clacher," she said and watched him leave the room.

FOURTEEN

Tor glanced at the items Ker had laid out for dinner. Should have been simple. Tor had told him he wanted a quick fix meal so he wouldn't look like a total idiot in front of Morgan. Instead, there were all kinds of spices and vegetables and was that a fucking pasta maker? Had Ker lost his goddamned mind?

He pulled out his cell to call his younger brother when he waltzed into the kitchen. "Hey, what are you doing in here?"

"I told you I wanted to make something for Morgan."

Ker snorted. "You did say that, but you don't cook. We both know that. You'd kill her if you tried."

"I made her grilled cheese," he growled in defiance.

Ker raised his brows. "Leave dinner to me. I was going to make fettuccini with lobster in pink sauce."

Tor frowned. "What?"

"The pasta dish you like so much, remember? With the lobster?"

"Oh, yeah. That's a good one."

Ker sighed. "Just set the table and pick out a bottle of wine." He glanced Tor up and down. "It wouldn't kill you to dress up once in a while. We have a gorgeous woman here eating with us and you're wearing this morning's outfit."

He ground his teeth together and snarled. "Fine. I'll go shower and change, and you cook."

Less than thirty minutes later, he was back from his shower to the delicious smell of food. Fucking Ker was showing off, baking fresh bread. And there was Morgan, smiling and laughing at Ker like he invented the food channel. He watched Morgan push her glasses up her nose, sending his hormones raging. He loved how innocent she looked with them on.

"Oh, look. Big bro is back." Ker made a face

when Morgan turned to glance at Tor.

He almost snapped Ker's head off but the look of pure desire in Morgan's eyes stopped him. She wanted him. He smelled her lust and it got to him on the most primitive levels. Even his dragon was affected.

"I feel so underdressed," she said softly, her gaze roaming up and down his body.

"Nonsense," Ker laughed. "You look gorgeous. That sexy schoolteacher thing really works for you."

She started giggling and Tor gave Ker a hard look. He mentally yelled at him for calling her sexy.

"Thank you, Ker. I've never heard that looking like a schoolteacher was sexy, but I guess times have changed." She sat at the dinner table where most of the meal was already set in silver serving bowls.

"Time to eat," Ker declared, bringing the croissants to the table.

There was a salad, pasta, and fresh baked bread. If Tor didn't know Ker was just a damn good cook, he would've felt like he was showing off.

They sat around the table and served themselves while they made small talk.

"Morgan," Ker said. "Tell me everything about you."

She grinned and the sparkle in her eyes loosened a knot in Tor's chest. "Like?"

"What's your favorite color? Where did you go to school? Do you have a boyfriend?"

Tor bit back a growl but managed to stay quiet and place food on his plate.

"My favorite color is silver. I went to a boarding school in Switzerland. I don't have a boyfriend," she replied and put a piece of bread in her mouth. She moaned and gasped. "Oh my goodness, Ker. I didn't realize this would taste so divine fresh out of the oven."

"Babe, put some butter on that and prepare to want to take me home with you," Ker winked.

Tor shoved some pasta into his mouth to keep from saying something rude. He knew what Ker was doing. Baiting him. Plus, he could see they were both getting along quite nicely without him having to say a goddamned word.

"I just might have to," she laughed. "Okay, your turn to tell me something about you," she said to Ker.

"What do you want to know?"

"What do you do for a living?"

Ker sat up straighter in his seat. "I own several

online antique businesses. I travel to multiple locations, track down any kind of storage places and buy them off whoever hasn't paid to get whatever's inside."

She squealed. "I've seen those guys on TV. Sometimes you can get a treasure, but sometimes you can get junk."

Ker glanced at Tor. "Tell her."

Tor rolled his eyes. "Ker has a sense for this. He doesn't buy just any storage. He researches before he does. And he sticks to buying really old houses that have been in families for generations with everything included. Then he sends a team to get rid of the crap and his people to go through the antiques."

She sipped on her wine. "But buying a house with everything in it. That would creep me out."

Ker grinned. "I don't keep the stuff. Actually, I never touch it. Once the trash is cleared out, I go in, bring my guys, the ones I've trained, and they categorize everything. Then we put it up for sale online."

"Sounds like a lot of work. How much could you possibly make from something like that?"

He shrugged. "A few hundred thousand to millions depending on what house and what family it came from. I'm very discerning. But this hasn't been my sole business. I learned antiques," he motioned to Tor with his head. "We all have due to our lifespan, but we've all had multiple jobs. Every hundred years or so, you get bored and need something new to try."

She turned to Tor. "Really?"

He nodded, swallowing the pasta in his mouth.

"What kind of stuff have you done in the past?" she asked Tor, a hint of a naughty grin on her lips.

"Him? He's been a knight, a warrior, merchandise importer, but most of all he's been a prince," Ker grinned. "A spoiled one at that."

"So no sultan or having a harem of women to choose from?" she asked, her brows high.

He saw the real question in her eyes. Had there been another woman in his life.

"No harem. Not a sultan. Just a dragon," he replied.

The conversation continued lightheartedly thanks to Ker. He had to give it to his brother, he wouldn't have been able to have this long of a conversation and dinner without getting her naked on the table and eating her pussy within the first ten minutes. The fucking image of her in that position made him clear his throat. He wanted to go back to her room and fuck her into his bedroom.

He didn't think she'd agree to that. At least not while they were still eating.

FIFTEEN

Morgan had never wanted so badly to forgo dinner and rush Tor back to her room to strip him down to nothing and cover him in kisses and her own body. He looked so good with those black jeans and the black T-shirt she knew he'd worn for her. The damn thing had a quote in the middle that read "It's Huge."

After dinner and amazing cups of chocolate mousse with whipped cream and wafers, Tor walked her back to her room.

"Tomorrow, I'll see if I can get anything on Ker," she said after a quiet moment. "I tried with Clacher earlier, but his dragon pushed me off."

They'd just reached her door and she was about to open it when he whirled her to face him. "Did he hurt you?"

She frowned at the rage in his voice. But it was the fear in his eyes that worried her. "No! I didn't mean to imply that. I meant mentally he pushed me off. He didn't want me poking at their bond."

He nodded, seemingly appeased with her words. "You have to promise to tell me if anyone harms you in any way. If anyone lays a hand on you…"

"Calm down, Tor," she said in the soft, soothing voice she used with her children clients. "I'm fine. Nothing happened." She realized he might need some time to cool off and as much as she hated to turn him away, she did. "I'm going to get ready for bed. I'll see you in the morning."

He searched her gaze and slowly pulled away. "Okay. Goodnight."

She was left alone in front of her door so fast, she wasn't sure what happened. She went into her room and checked her phone. Lexi had texted her, giving her a rundown of the day and asking about hers. She replied and much to her surprise, her mother had texted as well. She'd been polite in her past few texts asking how she was doing with Tor.

She told her things were great and kept it general. Her mother did not need to know Tor had fingered her by a river near his parents' cabin. Nope. That was totally unnecessary for anyone on the planet to know. Her mother wasn't being as cold as usual, and she wasn't sure why. Lara didn't message her this often and never asking how things were going.

She glanced around her room, finally taking in the décor and noticing there was a set of French doors she didn't notice before. She slipped off her glasses, finally happy to give her eyes a break and got up. She pulled the doors open to a balcony. The moon was full and she could almost see down the mountain to the river below.

Walking further to the side, she stopped when she realized there was another set of French doors. She glanced inside and saw Tor. Oh. Good. God. It was a very sexy, half naked, kill all her brain cells, Tor.

He wore a towel around his waist and nothing more. She gulped and watched him turn to face her. Oh shit. Oh fuck. He was going to catch her watching him like some perverted person that had no life. She stepped back and turned around, trying to move toward her door as quickly as possible. She was feet away when she heard him open the door.

"Stop."

Fuck!

She didn't say anything but her heart beat so loudly, she almost swore he could hear it.

"That delicious scent gave you away," he said

softly.

She had no idea what scent he was talking about. She'd forgone lotion so she wouldn't offend their sensitive sense of smell. "What scent?"

She finally pivoted on her heels and saw him standing with his arm on the balcony as he stared at her. "The scent of your arousal. It's fucking delicious."

Oh. That.

She couldn't help being hot for him. He was so damn sexy and after their little time by the river, she had a hard time not thinking of him being naked with her. "I'm...sorry?"

"Ah, baby girl. Don't be sorry," he replied and closed the distance between them. "Sorry is the last thing I ever want you to be for wanting me. For being wet for me."

She widened her eyes. "Wet?"

"I know you're wet." He approached her like a predator stalking his prey. "Don't bother denying it. I can slide my fingers between your pink folds and know they're slick for me."

She stumbled another step back. "That's quite a claim."

One she wasn't willing to deny. But she wasn't going to agree either.

His eyes glowed gold. "Fact. Not a claim. I also know your skin's hot from how turned on you are. No man has ever made you this hungry for more of what we had by the river." He was so close. She could almost raise her hand and touch that sexy face of his. "I'm taking more than your body tonight, Morgan." He took her hand and raised it to his lips.

"Tor…"

"Only your body will satisfy the raging lust and my need to fuck you until I come so deeply inside you, no one will ever question you're mine." He kissed her palm and rubbed it on his cheek. "Your heart? I'm not giving it back. It's mine. I can satisfy your every craving to be fucked like the goddess you are, but your heart is taken. It belongs to me, just like mine belongs to you now." He licked the tip of one of her fingers. "And your soul? It's already found a home with mine."

"Tor, you can't be serious."

"I am. I love every fucking gorgeous inch of you. Every generous dip and curve. Everything."

SIXTEEN

Morgan gasped. He curled a hand around her neck and pulled her toward him. His lips came crashing down on hers, twining and curling over each other like desperate animals in heat.

She might argue with him about the fact he was going to end up mated to some other woman, but for now, she wanted him for herself. She wanted him so damn badly. Even if only for a little bit.

There was too much going on inside her to think. She gave in to the raging need coursing through her veins. Her hands roamed his wet torso and yanked at the towel. Her mind filled with the image of what he'd done to her earlier. It was his turn to be pleasured.

His needs became hers. She pulled from their

kiss and dropped into a crouch, taking him deeply into her mouth. He groaned and gripped her long hair back, thrusting forward. "Morgan, fuck! You don't have to do this now."

She ignored him and continued. She'd been dying to taste him and now she knew he was delicious and bigger than she'd ever anticipated. He took up every bit of space in her mouth. She sucked hard, flicking her tongue under his shaft and jerking him at the same time. His groans of pleasure and the harder grip on her hair told her all she needed to know. He liked it.

Suctioning her cheeks tightly, she jerked him harder and faster, using her spit to lubricate him and add ease of sliding down her throat.

There wasn't much time to enjoy her work on his cock, he tugged on her shoulders and lifted her. Her clothes were shredded before she had a chance to ask why didn't he tell her to take them off.

She was then facing the balcony's ornate stone railing. He pushed her legs wide and knelt behind her. He tugged her ass back and within seconds his face was between her legs, his tongue draping up and down her pussy and up to her ass.

She squealed and pushed her ass into his face. She gripped the railing and felt her knees shake from the instant tension winding at her core. He continued flicking his tongue over her asshole and down to her pussy. He licked and thrust into her sex, fucking her with it.

Her moans and groans grew louder as he increased the speed and rotation of his tongue. She'd never met a man who could do the things he was doing. With his tongue or in general. She rocked her hips on his face, wiggling back and forth, looking for his tongue to go deeper. He pressed a finger over her clit and rubbed furiously from side to side. The intense heat that was already building inside her exploded into an all-out roaring blaze.

She screamed and her knees buckled but he held her upright, cupping her ass cheeks. Her pussy grasped at nothing for a second before he was there, thrusting his hard, slick cock into her.

"Fucking hell, you're still coming, aren't you?" He groaned.

She moaned, her pussy gripping and contracting on his cock as he thrust and retreated, quickly falling into a fast and hard rhythm.

"I've never wanted a woman like I want you," he growled.

"Oh yeah?" she asked, her lungs burning. "How's that?"

"Like I'd give my last fucking breath for you." He kissed the back of her shoulder. "Like if tomorrow never comes, I'd die a happy man because I got to spend tonight with you by my side."

She felt the first twinges of fire flaring at her center. The heat spread, consuming her with its power. Then she was blazing. A new hoarse scream lodged in her throat. The sense of pure bliss cooled the heat and took her body from boiling to a low simmer.

Her pussy grasped at his driving cock. He increased his speed. Harder. Faster. Until he was grinding his pelvis into her pussy, finally stopping when he came. He roared, his cock growing larger and taking every breath of space in her channel. He came deeply inside her, filling her with his cum.

Once he was done, he pulled out slowly and turned her to face him. He kissed her softly, claiming her lips as his once again. Then he picked her up in his arms and carried her to his bed.

"I like this Neanderthal side of you."

He chuckled and lowered her to the sheets, lying next to her and pulling her back in his arms. "I aim to please."

"All that stuff you said outside," she murmured.

"I meant every word."

She cleared her throat. "Tor."

"I wish you'd be able to look inside my heart. You'd see the truth to my words. I've gone a lifetime alone. A lifetime without someone I could love."

She bit her lip. "That's a long time."

"I'd give up every year I have of life just to spend another night with you."

"Don't say that! I can't imagine a situation where that would be necessary."

"It doesn't matter. I'd do it. I'd give everything to ensure you will always be mine."

She sighed and raked her nails down his abs. "Nothing is guaranteed in life."

"You're right," he said, his voice losing some of its strength. "Sometimes we don't have a choice when hard realities come to remind us we don't always get what we want."

She wasn't sure what he was referring to, but that reminded her that he'd find a mate soon and she'd be all but forgotten.

It was late at night when a vision woke her. She shot up in bed, her heart pounding at her throat.

"What's wrong?" Tor asked, his voice clear of sleep as if he hadn't been asleep a moment ago.

"My mother. Something's wrong. I dreamt she was being attacked by some of those black dragons."

"Dreamt?"

"Sorry," she shook her head. "It was more of a vision. I don't know what's going on, but I know that she's in trouble and she needs me."

She rushed over to her cell phone and dialed her mother. There was no answer. Her stomach clenched, nausea rolled up the back of her throat. "Oh, my god. It's bad. I sense it. I need to go to her."

Tor was already rushing into his jeans. "Don't worry. I'll get you to her in no time. Go get dressed."

She prayed her mother was fine and this sick sensation was just a bad dream and not a real vision. But she had a feeling there was something terrible happening to Lara. She had to get there. Her hands shook in her frantic haste to run to her room and get dressed. She could only hope she found her mother alive when she got there. Her instincts told her she wouldn't.

SEVENTEEN

"Lara?" Morgan called out, shoving the broken down door open. She almost lost her glasses when she tripped on a lamp. Her senses reeled. Pain gutted her from the inside. She could barely keep her legs from buckling. "Lara!"

She heard Tor behind her, trying to get past the furniture strewn all over the house. "I don't sense any Noir inside."

She gulped, hoping that whatever happened was just an accident. "Lara?"

A soft groan sounded from somewhere. She did a full circle looking for the noise and finally ran to a shelf on the floor. "Lara?"

She tried to move the piece of furniture but it was heavy. Tor rushed to her side and moved it like it weighed nothing. She dropped to her knees and pushed the books off Lara. "Are you okay?"

Lara met her gaze and winced. "I'll be fine."

"You're not fine. You have a lot of pain," she gasped, trying not to let the overwhelming sensations cripple her. "God, Lara. What happened?"

"I think we should get her out of here," Tor told her. He carefully picked Lara up in his arms and carried her out of the house, back to his SUV. "She'll be better protected at the mansion, but she really needs to be seen by a doctor. I know where to take her."

"How will we get there?" she asked. "I don't think she should be in a car for a long time. She needs medical help now."

"We'll take the helicopter. It's in a private pad not far from here and the private clinic I'm thinking of has a landing pad as well."

Lara passed out at that point. Morgan was glad for that in a sense. She knew her mother was in a lot of pain and it was devastating to know she could do nothing to help. "She's going to need a doctor soon. Will there be someone available to help her?"

"Don't worry," Tor replied back in the driver's seat. "I know who to call."

After what felt like forever, but must have been no more than forty-five minutes, they got to the private clinic. The building had guards and big gates. She didn't have time to wonder why, but made a mental note to ask later.

They were met outside by a medical team with a stretcher. Lara was rushed inside. Tor held her back, informing her that they'd let them know when they could visit with Lara.

She gulped, her chest felt tight and her lungs burned from how much it hurt to breathe. Lara was in so much pain. She could only hope her mother got relief soon. She'd never been able to feel her like she had this night.

"I can't believe she was attacked in her own home."

He curled his arms around her and pulled her in for a hug. She burrowed her face into his T-shirt and inhaled. The scent of man that was his alone calmed the frantic beating of her heart.

"I hate to say this, but I'm surprised they left her alive."

She gasped, glanced up and met his gaze. "What do you mean?"

"Sayeh and the Noir are not nice people. They don't care about anything but themselves and their sick need for revenge against us. Humans are pawns. They'd easily kill your kind without a second thought."

She allowed him to hug her tighter and pressed her head to his chest. His heart beat under her ear. The rhythmic sound gave her something to focus on. He glided his hands up and down her back, soothing away her fears. Though she'd spent her life locked out of Lara's emotions, she still cared about her. How could she not?

The woman was her mother. She remembered a time when she was a little girl and Lara had been loving and caring. Those were the brief memories she held on to every single day. If she didn't, she'd just have another reason to feel unwanted, something she refused to do.

She sat in the leather sofas in the waiting area next to Tor, holding his hand as if it was the most natural thing in the world. At that moment, it was.

"I hope she's okay," she sighed. "I haven't felt her pain in a while."

"I'm sure she will be fine. The hardest part is over, we got her here and she's alive," he told her, his arm going around her shoulders and squeezing her into his side.

"You know something?" she asked, glancing down at their entwined fingers. "I don't really know much about you, other than the fact you're a great kisser and amazing in bed."

He gave a soft growl and pressed a kiss to her temple. "What do you want to know?"

She glanced up at his eyes. There was a rim of silver around his dark irises. It gave him that beastly look she had become a huge fan of. "Tell me anything, but help me keep the worst scenarios out of my mind or I'll go crazy waiting for the doctor to come out."

"Okay. I've lived through many eras. One of my favorites was the eighteenth and nineteenth centuries. The clothing the women wore was much nicer than the stuff they use now."

She smiled and thought back to a movie she and Lexi had once watched. "Those long dresses like in Jane Austen?"

"Something like that. They were sometimes fluffy, but the necklines were low. Still, they were nice. The designs called more attention than what's used now."

"What else did you like about that time?" she asked.

"It was easier to shift, though it was harder to get clothes back on. Those breeches were a pain in the ass." He laughed. "It was easier to fly at night. There were no videos or planes or people looking for UFOs. It was simple."

"Wow," she shook her head, "I didn't realize

how difficult it must be for you guys now."

"It's not that bad, sweetheart. We are very careful, and for the most part, stay up in our mountain. We have our businesses and only deviate from our regular human lives when something important happens."

She grinned. "I still haven't been able to help you guys figure out anything about your mates."

"You've only been with us a few days. Give it time," he said and lifted the hand he had entwined with hers and tipped her chin back, lowering his head to give her a kiss she needed oh so badly. His lips brushed hers and peace glided over every cell in her body.

There was no urgency to the meeting of their mouths. He gave her warmth, strength through their touch. She wanted to say love, but the idea that a man she'd met just a few days ago could make her feel love was extra scary. She pulled back from their kiss, her heart racing and her blood pumping in her ears.

"I don't know that I can let you go, Morgan," he said.

She frowned. "What do you mean?"

EIGHTEEN

Someone cleared their throat and they both turned to see the doctor.

"Mrs. Polley is doing well. She's got some broken ribs, lots of bruising, and a sprained wrist and ankle, but otherwise, she'll be fine. We need to keep her here for a while. There's some swelling at the back of her head I want to monitor and to ensure no internal bleeding is happening." He smiled and glanced from Morgan to Tor. "She's asking to speak with you both. She's pretty heavily medicated for the pain, so she might not make much sense."

Morgan nodded and glanced at Tor. "Let's go."

Before they went inside, she tried to steel herself for her mother's emotions and pain. As she approached her, she got the sense that Lara was trying hard to bring back the wall she'd always kept around her emotions. Morgan could see the bruises on her mother's face much clearer now. There were black and blues forming on her jaw, finger marks around her neck and bruises on her arms. She felt like throwing up from just seeing that.

"I'm okay, Morgan," she said softly. "I know this is not a pretty sight, but I'm going to be fine."

"What happened?"

Lara glanced at Tor and then back at her. "I need to tell you some things, Morgan. Things I'm not sure you'll understand."

Morgan went around the bed and realizing her mother needed comforting, sat at the edge of the bed and held her hand. "You don't have to explain if you're not up to it. It's fine."

Lara smiled and shook her head. "No, baby. I have to."

The name took Morgan by surprise. Her last memory of Lara calling her baby was when she was four years old. That was a long ass time ago. "Lara, is everything okay?"

Lara's eyes filled with tears. "I've missed you calling me mom for so long," she choked out and squeezed at Morgan's hand.

What the hell was going on? Had she been hurt

worse than Morgan realized? "You have?"

Lara nodded. "When you were little, it was the most amazing thing. All you did was say mommy all day long."

"I don't understand what's going on here. My boarding school said calling you mommy wasn't appropriate and a term you didn't like."

Lara choked on another sob. "You were so small. And your abilities were too much for you. I didn't know what to do." She sniffled and gave Tor a slight nod when he handed her a box of tissues. "You don't remember, but your father died of a heart attack on a trip to the fair."

She frowned, racking her brain but coming back with nothing. She had no recollection of her father's death. She remembered him, but she only knew he'd died of a heart attack when she got older, never really getting all the details before. She knew from her mother's pain that she had no reason to lie to her about this. Everything she said was true. "I don't remember."

"I know." She cleared her throat. "When Michael fell to the ground in pain, you did the same. It was heartbreaking to see my daughter feeling the same pain her father felt as he died."

Dear god. A knot formed in her throat. She couldn't imagine seeing her child going through something like that. "But I don't remember."

"It doesn't matter. After losing your dad, I had a hard time with my emotions and you were paying the price. At first, I really thought I could handle it, but when my instability grew, I didn't know what to do.

"Your gift grew more with each passing day. I'd come home to find that you'd gone to the park and someone thinking of suicide had come too close to you. The pain you were in was…too much," she met Morgan's gaze, giving her a pleading look.

"One of your daycare teachers was being abused by her husband and things just got worse." She pursed her lips. "I called someone who'd been a lifelong friend of your father's. She mentioned she'd helped open up a boarding school that might be the place for you. Away from so much emotion and where you'd be able to grow up with less pain around you."

"You sent me away when I was four."

Lara nodded, devastation clear in her gaze along with regret. "I know. It killed me to do it, but then I realized this was the best thing I could do for you. I built my walls so when you finally came home, I wouldn't leak and you'd be able to come back to me. Except, you didn't want to come back."

She'd become best friends with Lexi and Amira. They had the same problem but Lexi's parents lived in Switzerland at the time, so when they took Lexi home on weekends they also took Morgan and Amira along with her. They became her family. When her mother tried to take her back years later, Morgan didn't want to go. Lara had rejected her once. Why would she want to be with her?

She wanted so badly to understand, but all she had were her childhood memories of wanting to go home and being told no. "I don't understand what this has to do with your attack tonight."

Lara lowered her gaze as if Morgan had struck her. "I'm sorry for sending you away, Morgan, but I did what I thought was best at the time. I missed you every second of every day you were gone. When you finally returned, you were so big and you didn't call me mom anymore. I'd sacrifice anything for you, but once you returned, you pulled further and further away from me." She picked up the glass of water on the bedside table and took a sip. "I became withdrawn and depressed. It helped me wall my emotions and keep you safe from the things I saw, the things I felt."

Morgan glanced at Tor. He hadn't said anything that whole time, just stood by and listened, his hand on her shoulder offering silent support. "Who attacked you? Why were you attacked?"

Lara inhaled hard and let it out slowly. "Big guy. Lots of tattoos. Dark, red eyes. They wanted to know where to find you."

"Me?" She gasped. "Why?"

"They want to kill you. You're special, and if you live, it means the beginning of an era of rebirth for the Drachen."

Morgan's eyes widened. "Because I'm helping them." Lara didn't answer. "I knew it. That's not going to stop me from what I'm doing."

"Tor will keep you safe until we know the next step," Lara said. "I just wanted to apologize to you. Maybe there was another way to do things, but I swear to you," she said and gripped Morgan's hands in her own. "I wanted to keep you safe. I wanted to keep pain away from you. You were so young. It wasn't fair."

Resentment and anger tried to make a home in her heart, but she pushed them away like she always had. She'd always known Lara was a good person. Not because of the emotions she hid from Morgan, but because of her aura. There was a light around her mother that she'd always been drawn to but kept away from so she wouldn't get hurt with Lara's rejection.

"You don't need to worry about me," Morgan said.

"That's right," Tor finally spoke up. "I'll make

121

sure she's guarded at all times."

She glanced up at him. "That's not what I meant."

"Too bad, that's how it's going to be," he replied. The authority didn't bother her. She sensed how worried he was about her so that was his way of taking control.

"I know," Lara said. "Thank you. Morgan," she squeezed her hand. "I'm here to answer any questions."

Morgan shook her head and frowned. "Why now? After all these years. Why?"

"I saw myself dying earlier. I'm not sure why I'm still alive, but I saw it happening and my one regret was letting this distance come between us. Allowing you to keep going through life without knowing how much I care about you."

That was kind of hard to believe at that moment when so many years had passed with Lara not once making a move to build a bridge between them. "Thank you."

Lara's eyes closed and opened less frequently.

"You get some rest. I'll be here," Morgan told her.

NINETEEN

After a while watching her mother sleep, the machines buzzing and beeping in the background, Morgan realized she needed someone to help take care of Lara. She had some urgent patients she had to see the next day. She brought her glasses up to the top of her head and wrinkled her nose. The view might be clearer, but her mind was still hazy.

In a daze, she left the room, slowly walking to a quiet spot down the hallway by the elevators. Nurse after nurse and doctors bypassed her without another word. The unit was especially quiet, but that was probably normal in an ICU.

She still couldn't wrap her mind around someone wanting to hurt her. Lara said they wanted to know where she was, but why?

Morgan had no enemies. Even her exes broke up with her in a nice way and they all tended to stay civil. They weren't friends, but nobody wanted her mom dead.

With a sigh, she leaned her head onto the window overlooking the outside. She saw the parking lot from that spot and thought about how she could help Lara. The only person who she felt comfortable talking to about that was probably asleep, but her best friend would understand.

She pulled her cellphone out of her pocket and dialed Lexi.

"Morgan," Lexis's sleepy-worried voice answered. "What's going on? How's everything going? What time is it?"

Nibbling on her lip, she tried hard to hold back the flood of tears clogging her throat. The things Lara had said…she'd hoped and dreamt for so long that one day her mother would tell her she loved her. But it had been so long of Lara holding back. Even though she'd known her mother wasn't lying, and dear god, she'd felt her pain, it was hard to ignore the years of rejection.

"Not so good," she murmured. "I just…I'm at the hospital with my mother. She was attacked and it's pretty bad." She sucked in a harsh breath. "I'm not sure what's going to happen to her."

"Oh my god, I'm so sorry. Is there something I

can do? Do you want me to come see you?" she offered quickly. "Just tell me where you are and I will get there as soon as possible."

She loved her friend.

"Actually, I was hoping you would be able to help me out. I can't watch her around the clock with some patients I have to see tomorrow. So I really need someone who can help me with making sure she's okay at the hospital."

"Of course, anything you need. Tell me where she's at and I'll come right over."

"Tomorrow's soon enough. I just wanted to make sure you could get some time off to help do this for me."

"Look, girl, I know you and your mother have always had issues, but you need me right now. I'm willing to do whatever is necessary. You're my best friend. I'm always going to be here for you just like you have been for me."

She gulped at the knot in her throat and brought her glasses back down on her nose. "Thank you so much. I can't begin to tell you what this means to me."

Lexi yawned and shuffling sounded from her side of the line. "How's everything going with Tor?"

She glanced around, knowing he'd gone to the waiting area to give her time alone with her mom.

"He's good. We've had a bit of a setback with this attack on my mother, and so far, I've got nothing from any of them. I don't even know what kind of help I am at this point. I want to keep trying though. The thought of his race dying out makes me sick." Better said, the thought of Tor dying because he couldn't find a mate was tearing her apart. "I'd like to see if I can get anything else."

Lexi was silent for a moment. "What aren't you telling me, Mor?"

Oh crap. She forgot Lexi knew her better than anyone in the world, probably even her mother. "There's some stuff I'd rather tell you in person," she said noncommittally.

"Okay. If that's the case, why don't you come over for a bit now and we can have a few hours talking and catching up."

"Hang on a sec, I have to see if I can," she trailed off and stopped the doctor attending her mom as he went by. "Excuse me?"

The doctor stopped and met her gaze. "Ms. Polley. What can I do for you?"

"How's my mom? Will she be regaining consciousness again tonight?"

The doctor gave a quick shake of the head. "We gave your mother some heavy pain medication and she'll be asleep all night and probably most of tomorrow. Please don't stay if you think she's

126

likely to wake. Go home. Get home rest and come back tomorrow. We'll take good care of her."

"Thank you, doctor."

She watched the doctor walk away not feeling any better about leaving her mother alone in a hospital when there was someone out there who tried to kill her.

"Okay," she finally said to Lexi. "I'll come by, but only until morning when I have to see some patients I'd intended on keeping on the schedule."

"Sounds good. Will Tor be okay with you staying here?"

She frowned. She never asked anyone for permission to go anywhere before. But she lived with Lexi so if he was worried about her safety, he could always stay over in their guest room. Or in Morgan's room, she'd never complain about that.

"I'm sure he'll be fine about it. Anyway, tell me about you. Let's not talk about me anymore. How are you doing? How's everything at the shelter?"

Lexi groaned. "I'm okay, things are pretty crazy at the shelter, but otherwise nothing I can't handle. I'm so happy that the family that I told you about, Jessica Santos and her kids? They're still with us and it seems like she's finally going to divorce her husband."

"That's great. It will be so good for the children to have a stable home environment without any violence."

"Yes. And she said she's going to keep him away from them. Seriously, Morgan. We can discuss this all later when you get here. Maybe go see your mom again and I'll get to cooking in the meantime."

Morgan's brows flew north. "You're cooking? But it's like 3 a.m."

"So? I'm starving now that I and my stomach are fully awake."

After she hung up the phone, she went to the other end of the hallway where the waiting area was. Tor stood inside, looking out a window at the darkness on ground level. She stopped at the door and watched him from there. There was something strangely soothing about him. Not just because they'd been incredibly intimate.

He had touched parts of her with just talking that nobody else had before. She was already half in love with him and it scared the crap out of her that in such a short time her feelings had gotten so involved.

The hardest and scariest part to swallow was that no matter what happened, she had to find him a mate. He needed a woman his dragon was compatible with and would spend eternity loving him. The thought alone stabbed at her guts.

She'd try to help him and his brothers find their mates meant to help them continue their race. She didn't know if she could stand the idea of giving Tor to anyone else. It turned her stomach to think of watching him fall in love with someone else. The very thought broke her heart.

He turned to face her, his eyes bright with his animal. Without saying a word, he walked up to her, pulled her into his arms and held her.

TWENTY

She should fight it or at least try to pull away. Her heart couldn't get any more attached to him. Who was she kidding? She wanted forever with a man meant for someone else. He might not be hers, not today, not ever, but she'd never turn from his touch. He gave her a peace she'd never found in any other man. With her emotions so raw, his arms were exactly where she wanted to be.

"How are you holding up?" he asked, sliding his hand into her hair and rubbing at the back of her skull. How he knew she had so much tension back there was beyond her.

"I'm good," she said, slipping her glasses off her eyes and pressing at the bridge of her nose. She shoved them in her bag, choosing not to wear them from the headache she felt throbbing at the back of her head. "Do you think she'll be okay?"

He inhaled and that pressed their bodies closer together. She heard his heartbeat, loud and strong, under her ear. He felt so good.

"Yes, I've spoken to the medical team and they will make sure she's back on her feet in no time. The doctor said she'd be asleep all night so it's best if you go home and get some rest." She heard the worry in his voice. "I know you probably don't want to leave her, but I can't leave you here. If you stay, I'll stay."

She shook her head and leaned back from his chest. "I'm going home to rest. Lexi's waiting for me and I'd hate to leave her waiting when I already agreed to come over."

"Okay. I'll take you to her."

He cupped her cheek and tipped her chin up so she could look into his eyes. "There's something we need to talk about. What I told you about doing anything to keep you is the truth, but I might not be able to and there's a reason. As much as would like to change things, there are powers stronger than me at hand."

"What are you talking about?"

"Your mother came to us because she wanted protection."

She gasped and widened her eyes in shock.

"What do you mean? I didn't realize she was in trouble."

He shook his head, his eyes bright with his dragon's fire. "She wasn't looking for protection for herself. She was hoping to get us to keep you safe."

She frowned and shook her head. "I don't understand. Why would I need protection?"

"Because Sayeh and the Noir attacked every single mate that has ever come to light and gotten the mate mark in our history and dwindled our species to only a few of us."

"I know, you told me that. It still doesn't explain why I would need protecting."

He stared deeply into her eyes, holding her so close, it was as if their clothes weren't there. "You're to get a mate mark. She saw it in her visions and knew your life would be in danger. So she called us so we'd protect you since you'll be getting the mark of one of my brothers."

"No!" She yanked herself away from him and stumbled back, her whole world reeling and rushing around her in sickening speed. "Your brothers?"

He nodded. "I'm sorry, Morgan."

"I have no marks," she murmured. "I can't be a mate. I would've seen it. Felt it. Something!"

He took a step toward her but she held a hand up. She couldn't allow her strained emotions to get out of hand. She'd tell him how she felt if he pushed just a little and she didn't need the pity.

He stopped and spoke softly to her. "You are. Your mother assured us what she said was true and I could tell if she'd been lying."

Her mother never lied about her visions. But why her? And who would she be mated to?

"I need to get out of here. I need to breathe."

"I'll take you home."

She nodded quietly and went outside where the hospital valet handed him a set of keys to his SUV. Someone from the private helicopter site had brought the vehicle over when they left it behind. She got in the passenger side and stayed quiet the entire ride to her home. Luckily, he didn't press her. She wouldn't have been able to handle anything else from him. Not when she wanted more than anything to be his.

When they got to her house, he pulled out his overnight bag and followed her inside.

"Hey!" Lexi rushed over from the kitchen to envelope her in a hug. She gazed worriedly into Morgan's eyes. "She'll be okay. I'm sure of it."

"The guest room is down the hall. Last door on the left. There's a bathroom attached," Morgan said without looking at Tor. He marched away in silence. She waited until his door had shut before she fell on the sofa and covered her face with her hands.

"Morgan, baby," Lexi whispered, her voice wobbly with tears. "What's wrong? What happened since I last spoke to you?"

"I'm one of their mates. It's why Lara wanted me to talk to them. It's why he's been protecting me."

"What?" Lexi gasped. She squeezed Morgan's hand and made her look up to meet her gaze. "How's that even possible?"

"Mom had one of her visions and instead of telling me about it, she called them to take care of me."

"Good god. Your mother just loves doing things backwards."

"Tell me about it. And he said I'm supposed to mate one of his brothers," she said, the lump in her throat growing with her words. "But how can I when…"

Lexi curled her arm around Morgan's shoulders. "When you're in love with him."

Morgan held back the tears, but that didn't stop the pain in her chest from making her feel like everything was being ripped out, leaving her hollow.

TWENTY-ONE

Tor felt like his world had ended. He needed her to know the truth of why he'd been protecting her. That didn't stop his feelings for her. He didn't know how to explain things better to her. He wanted to tell her that he didn't care who she was mated to, that he loved her and wanted her for himself.

But he did care. He'd never keep one of his brothers from their fated mate and the truth was once she got the mate mark, she'd feel the growing desire and love for her mate. It was a given. Besides, he'd never live with himself if he kept her and her mate apart only to watch them both die. He couldn't do it. Not to her and not to one of his brothers.

He didn't know what to do and at the moment couldn't stop to figure it out. She'd mentioned she wanted to go to her office to see clients so he'd stay in the vicinity. He knew her building was well guarded since she handled some very high profile clients and children of celebrities from around the world. They sent their kids to their small town so nobody would know they were undergoing therapy.

He dressed quickly and hurried to his vehicle to wait for her. Except she was already there waiting for him. She wore her hair back in a low ponytail and had a cream pantsuit on with flats.

She didn't meet his gaze, but he scented her sadness and it tore him apart. He shouldn't have said anything. He should've kept his mouth shut. She'd had enough to deal with already with her mother, but he knew she deserved to know.

Once they got to her office, he rushed to get her coffee and something to eat. He'd noticed she'd declined everything Lexi had offered to give her that morning while he got dressed. He dropped the food off at her office, noticing the smile on her lips even when she'd tried not to meet his gaze. A man and a little girl stood outside her door when he was walking out. He headed down to the lobby to wait out his time on the leather sofas and seating areas.

His cell phone rang and a quick look showed his brother had finally reappeared.

"Jae?"

"Tor, how's everything going with Morgan?" Jae asked without preamble.

He inhaled hard, thinking of how poorly he'd slept knowing she was a few doors down and he couldn't be there, holding her. "So far so good. She knows she's going to be one of your mates."

"*Your* mates?"

"One of the brothers."

"Not you?" Jae chuckled. "Do you not think she could be yours?"

He wanted to believe that so fucking badly but knew that would only lead to heartbreak if she wasn't. Best to get used to the idea of her belonging to one of the others now.

"No. Not me."

"You're still not over Sylvana, brother? You'd let her destroy your chance at happiness?" Jae asked with a sigh of frustration.

"We don't know whose mate she is. I don't want to grow attached to her," he lied. He'd grown more than attached. He'd fallen in love.

"Ah, Tor. You forget, I know you. I know the man and the dragon. You've kept Morgan all to yourself and growl at others who even look at her."

"Ker's a busybody," he growled.

Jae chuckled. "He is, but he loves you. We all do. Why can't she be meant for you?"

"I'd rather wait than get my hopes up."

"Your emotions are already involved and as far as I know, so are hers, so do yourself a favor, let someone else guard her until her mark shows up."

"No," he roared. The idea of going anywhere and someone hurting Morgan made him see red. "I can take care of her."

Jae sighed. "This won't end well, Tor."

He didn't give a fuck. He'd never felt one-tenth of the care and concern he felt for Morgan with Sylvana. With her he'd been young. All lust and sex. Morgan held his heart. Her body lured him but her innocence, her eyes, the purity of her soul captured his heart and trapped him. He'd fallen for the curvy therapist and he could only hope to enjoy every second they had together until she got her mate mark.

"How's your search for a mate?" Tor asked.

Jae growled his displeasure. "I don't know why I had a feeling to search this side of the world, but nothing has come of it. I did see a beautiful spot, quiet and solitary, perfect for a cabin."

"Let me guess, you bought it."

Jae chuckled. "You know it. The sight alone soothed my dragon. There were so many trees and foliage, I was able to lay out in my dragon without worrying about anyone nearby seeing anything. It's on a mountain. The beaches are fucking amazing. Wait 'til you see it."

Tor could imagine how the place looked. He'd traveled enough of the world to know the Philippines had beautiful beaches. They had a great many contacts in every country in the world they used for business. Money ruled and the Drachen family had enough of it. They might be running out of time to enjoy it, but they had a lot of money.

"I need you to stop by the bank," Jae told him. "Niko is waiting on you now. He's handling some new investments for us. Check out the paperwork and then sign if you think it's a good deal."

He glanced at his watch and knew Morgan's first client would be a few hours. He decided now was the time to do what Jae needed since Morgan was busy with one of the children. His gut told him to stay, but there was security all over the place. She'd be fine for a short while.

TWENTY-TWO

Morgan sat across from Isabelle and spoke to the little girl who'd become like a daughter to her. Her own body reminded her she needed kids soon. She wanted them badly and the urge only grew with time.

"How has it been at the new house, Isabelle?"

Isabelle shrugged in her little black cardigan and swung her Mary Janed feet on the sofa. "Okay, I guess. Aunt Sara tries really hard to make me feel comfortable."

She sensed Isabelle was holding back and understood. Having been abducted twice due to her father's high profile job and net worth, plus watching her mother get killed trying to stop the abductors had really destroyed the child.

"Where's Daddy, Isabelle?" she asked and

140

took notes. "Is he still not coming to see you?"

She shook her head and the flood of pain the child felt at that moment almost choked Morgan. She put her pad down and got down on the rug, pulling the little girl into her arms. Shoving her glasses up over her head, she made an effort to hold Isabelle tightly to her. "I'm sorry, baby. Your daddy loves you, Isabelle. He's scared of anything else happening to you. He doesn't want to lose you."

Isabelle sobbed into Morgan's suit jacket. "I wanna see my dad."

Morgan nodded. "I'll make it happen, baby."

She held Isabelle while the child cried her little heart out for long moments until she finally ended in soft, quiet hiccups. "Doesn't he want to see me?"

"Oh, baby, yes. He loves you and wants to see you but when adults get scared, they do stupid things, thinking they are protecting the ones they love," she said, thinking of her own mother and how she'd sent Morgan away, hidden her away and locked her feelings up because she thought it was best.

A knock on the door indicated the end of the session. Morgan helped Isabelle clean up before she went back to her driver who waited at the door for her.

Once Isabelle was gone, she marched to her desk and picked up the phone to dial the little girl's father. He'd made it very clear he'd be available for anything she needed at any time. He wanted his daughter to be safe and hopefully forget the trauma from the abduction.

Morgan had been able to slowly help Isabelle put the pain and memories into a box at the back of her mind. She still had knowledge of what happened, but the pain had been dulled and the memories made hazy. It was her father's lack of visitations that hurt the child more than anything.

"Ms. Polley, this is Kevin Malcolm. What's happened? Is Isabelle okay?"

She heard the genuine concern in the man's voice, which made this easier, but she knew he was scared for Isabelle. She'd felt his fear the moment of her first meeting with him. Like a pair of hands choking out the air from her lungs and every time she managed to get any oxygen in, it was a foul and bitter scent.

"Mr. Malcolm, I just want to tell you that Isabelle needs you. She misses her father and her therapy is otherwise going very well."

"I don't know if it's a good idea for me to go over there. What if they find her again?"

"Mr. Malcolm, I'm going to make this very clear. You're seeing your daughter. You're going to make arrangements for her to live with you again and you're going to do this because I know you love her." She took a deep breath and turned to glance out her glass window. "I know you have her best interest at heart, which is another reason why you're going to do this. Isabelle's therapy has been going so well, but her missing you reminds her every single day of her loss of her mother. If you truly love your daughter, you're going to take her back with you."

"Ms. Polley, I just don't want to lose her again," he choked. "With my wife gone, she's all I have left."

She swallowed hard, she expected this. "Kevin," she said softly, "she needs *you*. She loves you so much, and she thinks you forgot her. That you don't want her near you. Trust me, you don't want her to grow up with that as her reality. Because even if you know it's not true, it will be true to her."

"I love Isabelle."

"I know. That's why I am telling you, please, come visit her and take her home. But I have some requests. You need to spend alone time with her, here, at the house with her aunt. You can't just come take her back. She needs to trust that you want her with you again. She needs to know you love her and you genuinely want her to be with you."

"But—"

"No buts, Kevin. You'll hire the best of the best to guard your house and you'll ensure she has the ability to be a kid, because living in a prison, no matter how beautiful, is still a prison. She needs to be a kid. To have fun. To play. To be loved by her dad. Let her see that she might have lost Mom, but you're going to love her twice as hard for the both of you. She needs it. You need it."

"I'll fly in tomorrow."

"Thank you, Mr. Malcolm. This is the best thing you can do for her. Trust me. She will heal a lot better knowing she's got your love and support."

"Thank you, Ms. Polley. I will do that."

"Have a great day, Kevin. She'll love seeing you."

She hung up the phone lightheaded, shaken and weak. Her back felt hot. Nausea rolled up her throat. She hated feeling so vulnerable but this was normal with clients in pain. She felt their pain and it took a toll on her.

She had a half hour between appointments. It would take that long to get herself back to normal. Sitting on her office chair, she turned to face the window that overlooked the back alley and the forest not more than two streets away.

Her mind tried to get her thinking about Tor

and what it could mean for her to be one of his brothers' mates. She refused to give that thought another moment. Not when she was so shaken already.

She sent a text to Lexi to make sure all was okay with her mom. Lexi replied just as quickly and told her she'd been sleeping and they'd given her more pain meds when she mumbled about everything hurting.

Someone knocked at her door. She glanced at her clock. She still had twenty minutes before her next appointment.

She got up to open the door but once she got there, something told her not to open it. She rushed back to her desk when the door slammed open, the wood hitting the wall and bouncing back.

TWENTY-THREE

Morgan glanced over her shoulder at a guy standing there. He wore all black, his eyes a deep burgundy and his skin the color of gold. She got to her desk and grabbed her phone but he was there, knocking it out of her hand before she got a chance to press a single key.

He picked her up by the front of her jacket, shaking her to the point her glasses fell from her face. "My mistress wants to meet you."

"Oh, really?"

His eyes blazed a fiery red with flames licking at his irises. "Yes, she does. We can do this the easy way, or the hard way."

She ground her teeth and slammed her knee into his crotch. "The hard way, asshole! Something you might never be again!"

He dropped her and doubled over in pain. She heard him gagging as if he was going to throw up. She winced and tried to ignore his pain. Block it out. Just block it out. She'd hit him as hard as possible, not caring for his ability to conceive for the rest of his life.

She crawled around him, trying to reach the phone he'd knocked out of her hand. She finally jumped to her feet, unsure where the damn thing landed and ran for the door. She yanked the door to the stairs open and hauled ass down the three flights.

A loud roar sounded at the top of the stairwell and she knew a very pissed off black dragon was coming her way. She ran to the lobby but none of the security were anywhere to be found. The phone had been ripped out of the reception desk. Goddammit!

Morgan ran outside and felt her heart stop in her chest. A van started speeding toward the front of the building. Not a single fucking person was outside at that time. She'd known the area was quiet with everyone in their offices during business hours, but dammit this was surreal. She remembered the deli around the block she always went to for coffee and knew there would be someone there.

Fuck. Now what? She darted around the corner and started crossing the alley, uncaring of the puddles of water splashing on her cream pants. She was halfway down the alley when someone landed in front of her, stopping her movement to get to the deli not twenty feet away.

It really wasn't her day. She did the fastest U-turn known to man and almost landed on her ass trying to get away from the guy that somehow got from the damn stairs to the alley ahead of her. Fucking dragons and their super powers.

At that moment, she wished she had some kind of bat signal to get a hold of Tor. She got to the side of the alley she'd come from and stopped just in time to see the van being engulfed in flames. She gasped and glanced at Tor in his dragon of blue scales shooting and targeting fireballs at the van and those that ran out of it.

The guy behind her was no longer there. There was a pile of shredded clothes on the ground and then a big shadow went above her head.

She couldn't believe how much bigger Tor's dragon was compared to the black and red one. The guy's flames were tiny compared to Tor's. She was scared but wished she could grab something and beat the motherfucker down for making her run. She was still trying to catch her breath.

The fight was on. Tor's dragon was angry. She could see it in the color of his scales, the blue tinged with orange. He sent missiles at the black who did a bang up job of dodging them and making some of them hit signs and buildings by changing course at the last second. The guy was clearly well aware of how the Drachen fought.

He came back with a quick attack, shooting blaze after blaze of red fire at Tor but she didn't hear him or feel him have any pain. Tor shot into the sky, pushing far and fast. The black followed. Then he headed east, so fast and far she couldn't see them any longer. She didn't know what was going on, but she couldn't mentally reach out to know if either was in pain.

She glanced around the empty streets, the van was on fire and people suddenly came out of buildings, looking for whatever was making the racket. The sound of sirens came from down the road. Fire trucks surrounded the exits and stopped all traffic, not that there was any to begin with. Still, no sign of Tor.

Her heart bled from the thought of him being hurt. She couldn't believe he'd left only to get killed somewhere she couldn't help him.

She ran inside her building, looking to get away from the police officers asking questions and the curious onlookers. Already some were staring at her weird for her dirty, torn suit.

Upstairs, she waited what felt like an eternity, staring at her cell phone. She'd found it and her glasses on the floor, not too far from her desk. Her door creaked. Her gaze shot up and there he was, his clothes on haphazardly, but alive.

She jumped to her feet and flew into his arms. There was no hesitation. No questioning. She thanked every deity in the universe for his safety and met his gaze. There was so much anger in his eyes, anger and fear. Which she knew well didn't belong together but she could almost feel his worry like her own.

"Are you okay?" his voice was low and rough, like it had been run through sandpaper.

"Yes, you?" She gulped. "I was so scared when you flew away and I couldn't see you."

He held her closer and once again, the warmth in his body soothed the chill in her bones. "I'm fine. I knew I couldn't stay and kill him here, not near you."

She frowned. "Why not?"

He cupped her cheek and kissed her forehead. "I couldn't bear to see you suffer through his death."

"I saw you get hurt several times with his fire balls but I couldn't sense it."

"I blocked it so you wouldn't feel what I felt. I don't ever want to know you are hurting. I'll do whatever I have to do to stop it. Even if I have to block my pain to my last breath."

She felt her lip quiver and kissed the hand cupping her jaw. "I wish I knew what to do."

His shoulders slumped and for just a fraction of a second, she felt the pain of knowing he loved her but couldn't have her. It was devastating.

"Your mark and your mate's will show itself soon. Then we'll know."

She shook her head. "I already love you," she admitted stubbornly. "I won't magically fall in love with some other guy because a tattoo shows up on my skin."

"You can't fight the mate bond, love. Your love for your mate will grow and it will consume you." His eyes glowed pure gold. "Until all you want is your mate, your family with him and no one else will matter. Not anyone in the past."

She didn't know what to say, so she stayed quiet and let the moment hang in the air. "I need to change and come back for another client I have tonight. Last minute."

He nodded. "Let's get you home. I'll bring you back later."

TWENTY-FOUR

Once they got to her house, she got rid of her glasses, took a shower and glanced at the clock on her bedside table. They had a few hours before she needed to go for that last minute appointment. Under the circumstances, she was tempted to call and cancel, but she knew her client needed closure and a last moment of peace.

She padded down the hallway to knock at Tor's room door. He opened up wearing nothing but a towel. The image of where that got them last time flew to the front of her mind.

"Everything okay?"

"Uh, um," she glanced at the water drops crawling down his body, disappearing into the towel and only god knew down to where. Though, she could imagine. "Yes. Fine. I just wanted to tell you I'm going to take a nap. I know you didn't sleep last night, I heard you walking around and was hoping you'd take the time and get some rest, too. After the ordeal at my office, I feel like you need some healing time."

He gave a sharp nod, his gaze taking in her tank top and shorts. "That sounds like a good idea. I'll do better if I do get rest now."

She walked backward, hesitantly. If only she could change the future. If only she could know who her future mate was, then maybe she would be able to figure out where to go from there.

She'd been in bed, dozing in and out of sleep when her cell buzzed. She picked it up, wondering if it was her mother or Lexi.

Sure enough, the text was from Lexi.

> M: Come to the hospital asap. Don't bring Tor. There's something about him you need to know. He's been lying to you. He already has a mate.

Her heart froze in her chest. Could it be possible? She sucked in a hard breath. She'd known Lexi all her life. She was her best friend. She'd never lie to her. If she said Tor was mated, then he was the liar.

She slipped clothes on and got the new car keys Tor had given her earlier, leaving as quietly as possible without waking him. She couldn't go back for her glasses now. Luckily, she could still see, just not as clearly as she did with them on.

She was trying to think of why he'd tell her he had no woman or why he wasn't mated, when a van came up her side, got in front of her and stopped, making her hit the brakes.

She recognized the men coming out of the van. "Is everything okay, Rusty?"

"It's my wife, you have to come now. She won't last 'til tonight."

She wanted badly to say no, but her empathy stopped her. Rusty's pain and his worry for his wife were real. "Okay, I'll follow you."

He looked like he wanted to argue with her, but nodded. She proceeded to follow the black van down the road and straight to a main street. She texted Lexi she'd be there later. First she'd see about Rusty's wife. The woman wouldn't live long. If only she could help her go in peace, then it would be worth any pain she had to endure.

Half an hour later, her back burning like someone had struck her with a hot poker, she got out of her car at a deserted farm. The old farmhouse was caving in on itself. She could see the beauty it had once been and knew it had fallen to a slow death, like Rusty's wife.

Rusty took her inside to a room on the first floor. The room was tidy and full of wild flowers in different vases. A very frail woman, her head covered in a silk scarf, lay in the center of the four poster bed.

Morgan's back burned like someone was lighting a fire back there. She winced at the pain but rushed to the chair by the woman's side and grasped her hand between hers. The woman opened her eyes. "Am I dead?"

Morgan shook her head. "No, Helena. You're not dead. I'm here to offer you some comfort."

Helena glanced past Morgan at Rusty. "Thank you."

He cleared his throat. "I would give my life for yours if I could."

Helena smiled. "That's not necessary, darling. In time, we'll be together again."

"Tell me about your marriage," Morgan asked Helena.

"I met Rusty when we were both little kids. For a long time, I had no idea he even knew I existed, until I turned sixteen." She chuckled, her laughter turning into a bout of coughs.

"Sixteen is definitely the age where boys realize girls should get their attention." Morgan grinned, patting Helena's hand and rubbing circles over the protruding veins.

"We've been together since. I could never give

him the children he wanted, but he didn't care." She met Morgan's gaze. "I had cervical cancer at only twenty and had to have a hysterectomy. He always said I was all the family he needed." Her eyes watered. "Until the cancer returned. Now he'll be all alone."

Morgan could sense Rusty's pain at her back along with the fear in Helena of leaving him alone.

"I am not letting you go anywhere, sweetheart. We still have many years to live."

"Oh, Rusty," Helena gasped. "I love you, but you can be so dense."

Morgan ignored the fire blazing at her back, ignored the sweat gathering at her upper lip and focused on Helena. On her pain. She pulled at it, soothing where she could and almost massaging the balls of torture the poor woman was dealing with.

Helena gave a small sigh of relief and closed her eyes. Her previously labored breathing calmed. Morgan turned to Rusty, sadness clogging her throat. "You were right. She won't last long. I'll stay in the house until she's passed."

"Come, I'll make us some coffee." Rusty marched out of the room. She stood and walked after him, closing the door behind her.

In the living room, she stopped when she saw

the front door open. The other man from the van, she didn't get his name, was there.

"She's here," the tattooed man said.

"Adonis," Rusty said. "I never told you it was okay to bring her."

Adonis. Morgan eyed the big guy with the tattoos, piercings all over his head and face, and decided his name was clearly not well thought out.

"You wanted someone to cure, Helena!" Adonis hissed. He eyed Morgan with an evil glare. "All I had to promise the witch was this girl. You were already bringing her here. Two birds. One stone. Get it, old man?"

Morgan's back finally eased up. She was glad because it seemed she was in some kind of trouble and she'd left her cell phone in the car in her rush to get to the dying Helena.

"She helped Helena rest. For the first time in months, she fell asleep without pain, Adonis!"

"It's too late to change anything. Sylvana is already here."

Morgan glanced at the entrance where a new person walked in. She was tall, slim and beautiful with raven long hair and eyes. Her gaze found Morgan and stayed there.

"So, you're the one," the woman said in a soft,

flinty voice.

"The one?" Morgan widened her stance, realizing this woman was evil not just from her aura, but from what she saw. Something Morgan had never experienced in her life happened then. She saw the past. She saw Sylvana's past. The images were so fast through her mind, they were almost in a blur. Until it got to her and Tor. Then it was like watching a movie on fast forward. She saw, heard and captured everything as if she'd been there herself.

"Tor's new play thing."

Morgan grinned. "No. I'm not his new play thing. He's an amazing man, but I would never play with him or his emotions."

Sylvana raised her hands and shoved everything, people and furniture, out of the surroundings, leaving a large open space where only she and Morgan stood. This was the witch. The witch the crown had been made for.

"You *are* his mate, little human." Sylvana gave a perfect evil smile. "Yes. I see you are surprised. It's the truth. You and Tor. But now that will never happen because I'm here to get rid of you. Tor will never know happiness. Ever."

"You never said she was going to kill her!" Rusty yelled at Adonis.

"How the fuck was I supposed to know? And

what does it matter anyway? If she can save
Helena?"

TWENTY-FIVE

Morgan shook her head and stared at the witch. Morgan should be afraid. She knew that, but something told her not to worry. That it would all be fine. "She won't help Helena, Rusty. I'm sorry. She's only here to kill me." She glanced at Adonis being held back by a pile of furniture. "And you, too. She knows Rusty's death will be watching the love of his life die."

"Very good, little empath," Sylvana said. "Now tell me something else. Has he fucked you?"

Morgan raised her brows. "I don't really think that's any of your business."

For the first time since she arrived, Sylvana showed her emotions. Fury lit her eyes into pools of red. "*He* is my business. He's been mine and will never know another woman as long as he lives."

She stared into Morgan's eyes. She could feel Sylvana prodding inside her head. She was about to tell her to get out when her mind built walls. First in stone. Then in concrete. Then brick. Wood. Massive walls built in her mind to stop the witch from digging into her head.

"Build all the walls you want, little empath. I already know he fucked you." Sylvana raised her hands again and a circle of fire surrounded them. Someone whispered in Morgan's mind. She struggled to listen until she realized it was her Tor.

"Focus on the furniture and move it, Morgan."

"Tor?"

"You can do this. Move it. Hit her or she will kill you before I get there."

She wanted to ask how he was in her head or how he knew where to find her, but instead she focused on a big handmade dining room table that looked to weigh a few hundred pounds. It was on its side. The table trembled the longer she stared at it.

"She's going to kill all of us if we don't get out of here," Adonis said to Rusty.

"I'm not leaving this woman behind, not when she helped me. Besides, Helena is in bed, plugged into the painkillers!"

"Suit yourself," Adonis yelled and tried to head up the stairs. She saw his intent. He was going to try and jump over the railing on to a sofa so he could reach one of the windows closest to him. He was suddenly pulled back down.

"You aren't leaving us so fast," Sylvana said to him. "Are you?"

Morgan shut off all the conversation and noise and called the table to fly. It moved so fast, zipping into the air flying at the witch, she almost missed it. The table hit Sylvana on the side, knocking her off her feet.

Sylvana glanced around, looking for the culprit. The earth started shaking. Loud screeching sounds came from the ceiling. Morgan knew that noise. She covered the top of her head and watched as the roof of the house was peeled back by a massive orange dragon.

A loud roar sounded and wings flapped as it shook the house, trying to bring it down.

Sylvana turned to face the large dragon, her hands raised, but Morgan's mind connected with him before he continued destroying the house.

"Stop, Tor. There's a dying woman here. If you destroy this house, you'll kill her."

He pulled back, still flying above them. Then a black dragon slammed into the orange one and

Sylvana was back to facing Morgan.

"Let's end this. It was already a piece of cake to get you away from Tor. Who do you think sent you those messages? It wasn't your little friend."

Morgan gasped. She'd gotten her to leave Tor, her protector, behind so she could come here and get to her alone. She felt so stupid. "Did you hurt Lexi? What did you do to them?"

Sylvana laughed. "I have no need for your friend or your pathetic mother. I only needed you to think she messaged you."

"Why do you want to kill me?"

"If you die, Tor will never have a mate."

She nodded. "But killing me will also kill him."

Sylvana stopped to think for a moment but then shrugged. "I'll miss him, but I'll find someone else to torture."

Morgan tried something new with her sudden mental power. She shoved at the witch with her mind. Sylvana flew back, breaking the front door down and landing outside. The fire she'd started at the center of the living room went out the moment she landed on her back.

Morgan rushed outside, hoping to keep her away from Helena and destroying the house.

Sylvana was already on her feet, hands raised and calling on her powers. Fuck.

"Call on the fire balls," she heard Tor say in her mind. *"Think of the fire balls and shoot them at her."*

She was running out of time. Sylvana had the ground shaking. Morgan thought back to the balls of fire she and Tor had discussed. His dragon controlled them with his mind. What if she could control some with her mind, too?

She visualized massive fireballs in orange and they materialized at the palm of her hand. She gasped, unsure what the fuck was going on but willing to go with it. She pointed at Sylvana, who was ready to kill everyone in that area when the fire balls shot out of her hands and hit the witch on either shoulder.

Sylvana was knocked out of her power call. She roared and sent lightning bolts toward Morgan. She didn't have time to move, but the bolts never hit her. Her dragon mate was back. Tor landed in front of her, stopping the electrical charges from hitting her. He took the hit hard but continued to protect Morgan.

Sylvana screeched. "You can't protect her forever!"

Tor's dragon sent fire blades straight at Sylvana. She tried to wave them off, sent her own blazing balls, but they continued until they got their target. The blades slammed into her, lighting her on fire.

The dragon didn't stop. He continued his attack on the witch. Even as she tried to run from him. Until there was only smoke and she was gone. Morgan couldn't tell if she'd burned to death or had done a disappearing act.

She watched her dragon once again land. He shifted into his human body and ran to her. She jumped at him, uncaring of her size or weight. All she knew was that this was her man. That she wouldn't have to give him up because he was her mate.

They kissed like they'd been given a second chance at life. In a way, they had. They could be together and not worry about her being mated to one of his brothers. She rubbed at his shoulders and frowned, pulling away from their kiss when she felt a scar that hadn't been there before.

"Hang on a second," she said. "Put me down."

He did as she asked. She walked around him, seeing for the first time the mate mark on Tor. There it was, a massive dragon tattoo with her initial on its wing.

She realized then that the burning she'd been feeling at her back must have been her own mark making itself known. It would be interesting to see what hers looked like. Later, after they helped Helena see to her last breath with Rusty by her side.

Rusty ran out of the house with a robe for Tor. "Please," he called to Morgan. "I know I don't deserve your help after what happened, but I never wanted you to get hurt. I only wanted my Helena to have another chance at life."

Morgan shook her head. "Don't worry. I understand. I'm sorry you didn't get your wish of her getting more time here with you."

"It's fine. I just want her last moments to be at peace. Can you help?"

She nodded. They went inside to help Helena spend a few moments of peace with the man she loved.

TWENTY-SIX

Morgan wrapped her robe around her waist and grinned at her body in the mirror. She touched her already rounded belly and chuckled. That wasn't the baby, not yet. That was just her very curvy body, but soon, it would be all her baby. Her month old baby grew inside her. She couldn't believe her little dragon had been blocking everyone from knowing his existence until now. She could only imagine what that meant for his powers.

Wait 'til she told her mate. She left the bathroom and caught him by the same balcony where they'd first made love. The one they'd made their baby on.

He turned and marched right up to her, taking her into his arms and kissing her. Their lips melded and joy flowed in her heart. She kissed him back, a new bond growing tighter and stronger between them. She could see into his mind and heart and knew he felt the same.

Then there were his powers. They grew stronger since their mate marks showed. He could now see the future where she could see the past. They were both getting used to their new powers and visions. As it was, Morgan no longer needed glasses to see. Their mating changed both their lives.

Morgan shoved his pants down, immediately curling a hand around his length and pumping him. He groaned into their kiss and tugged at the tie around her waist. He pulled her back as he sat on the edge of the ottoman at the foot of their bed.

He slipped the robe open and kissed her breast, sucking a tight peak into his mouth. His hot tongue curled around her aching nipple and gave a gentle tug. A soft moan left the back of her throat. She leaned forward, gripping his shoulders and straddling him. He slid a hand between her thighs, fondling her clit and dipping into her channel.

He let go of her breast and inhaled at her tit. "Something's different about you, sweetheart."

She groaned and rocked her hips on his hand. "That I'm standing?"

"No," he growled and drove his fingers deeper into her sex. "Lord, you're soaked. I fucking love it."

"I fucking love your tongue, Tor. God!"

He licked from one nipple to the other and bit between them. "Your scent," he grunted between bites, "is different."

"Shut up and fuck me already," she panted, pulling his hand from between her legs, grabbing a hold of his cock and sliding down. She took him in one fell swoop. She was wet and ready. Her body shook with how badly she ached for him. He was big, but she accommodated him easily.

"Christ, baby. You're extra tight this time."

She could imagine. He felt extra massive. He grabbed at her ass cheeks and licked her collar bone. "I love you."

She curled her arms around his neck and kissed his beard. "I love you, too, you big, sexy dragon."

She rocked on him, back and forth at first, then she pressed her knees into the ottoman and lifted and dropped over his cock.

"You're always going to be mine, Morgan," he told her. "All mine. You were mine before I knew you were my mate."

He gripped her hips and helped her ride him.

Her chest burned from lack of air, but she managed to reply. "I love that I loved you before this mate mark came along. I might have not known for sure if it was the mark or true love."

He shoved her down harder. Faster. His moves increasing with his breaths and grunts. "I'm glad you know I loved you before the mark as well. I fucking love you to the ends of the earths, baby girl. Mark or no mark."

She gulped, feeling her body tighten as she readied to fly. "I know, Tor."

He pushed her down and ground her against his pelvis. Then he pressed a finger between her folds, right at the heart of her pleasure. She groaned and continued riding him.

"Your pussy, your curves. Every fucking part of you is mine. Will always be mine."

She kissed all over his face. He pressed a kiss by her ear. "There will never be another woman that makes my dick hard and my heart soft like you do. Not in this lifetime and not in the next."

She came then, her body bowing and pressing forward, her pussy contracting around his length. Pleasure consumed her, rushing through every limb and exiting through every pore.

He joined her in her climax, groaning and spilling his seed into her already fertile channel. He pulsed inside her, dragging another orgasm from her shaky core. "I fucking love you, Morgan."

"I'll never stop loving hearing you say that. I love you, too, Tor."

EPILOGUE

Tor left his wife sleeping. He knew if he didn't hurry, she'd wake and take care of baby Noah. Who would've thought there would be an actual argument over who would change a diaper in the castle. He usually lost to her or Ker, but tonight he'd been waiting for her to fall asleep so he could sit with his son for a while.

He entered the connecting room they'd turned into a baby suite. Little Noah was already gurgling and waving his tiny fisted hands madly in the air. He wasn't in need of a change, but Tor would have felt bad waking his son otherwise. Now, he could hold him without worrying about waking him.

He picked up Noah and lifted him into his arms. Then he sat in the rocker Morgan had insisted was needed. He was glad he'd given into every desire for the baby suite because he loved the rocker. It was his favorite spot to sit with Noah and look out the window.

"How are you, son?"

Noah gazed at him with his big golden eyes. A chubby toothless smile on his lips. The baby coo'd and aah'd.

Noah looked exactly like Tor. He smiled and Noah smiled as well. There was a deep bond between them, something he'd never felt before and wouldn't have known how amazing it was until after he had his son. For so long, he denied himself the hope that one day he would have a mate and children, but now he realized why he'd done that.

One can't miss what one never had. Except now that he had both, he'd never in his life deny how special they were to him. Morgan brought him into the world of the living. He'd been existing before. Now, now he was alive. And no way was he missing a second of it.

The door creaked open. He glanced up and met Morgan's gaze.

"Hey, sexy," she whispered. "I see you finally got ahead of me."

He chuckled and crooked a finger to call her to him. "Get over here. You are tough to beat. I don't know how you always know when he's going to be awake."

"Instinct." She sighed and took the baby from his arms then settled on his lap.

"You're one of the most loving and forgiving women I've ever met."

She groaned and wrinkled her nose. "What did you do? Why are you saying that?"

"I was just thinking about your mother and how much you let go in order to rebuild your relationship with her."

She shrugged. "What's the point of holding on to all that pain? Besides, I know she loves me and I want Noah to get as much love as possible from all family members."

He nodded. "See. You're beautiful. Inside and out. And you have some kind of power that you know when our baby needs something."

"I never realized what other mom's meant when they said instinct from the beginning, but our baby calls to me when he needs something."

Tor brushed a finger over Noah's chubby cheek. "Well, he better start calling on me, too. I'm his father."

She laughed and kissed his head. "This just means we'll need to have another so you can help out more."

His heart filled with love for his wife and child. He was the first of his family since arriving on earth to keep his mate alive long enough to have offspring and give it life. Now his brothers needed to do the same. It was only a matter of time. Soon, they'd all have families. He knew it deep in his heart.

"Let's go, mister sexy dragon," she whispered. "Noah's asleep."

"Good. Let's make him a sister."

Tor watched her put the baby down and picked her up in his arms, carrying her to their room.

"Have I told you how much I love this Neanderthal side of you?" she asked.

"Every time I pick you up."

THE END

ABOUT THE AUTHOR

New York Times and USA Today Bestselling Author

Hi! I'm Milly Taiden. I love to write sexy stories featuring fun, sassy heroines with curves and growly alpha males with fur. My books are a great way to satisfy your craving for paranormal romance with action, humor, suspense and happily ever afters.

I live in Florida with my hubby, our boys, and our fur children "Needy Speedy" and "Stormy." Yes, I am aware I'm bossy, and I am seriously addicted to iced caramel lattes.

I love to meet new readers, so come sign up for my newsletter and check out my Facebook page. We always have lots of fun stuff going on there.

SIGN UP FOR MILLY'S NEWSLETTER FOR LATEST NEWS!

http://eepurl.com/pt9q1

Find out more about Milly Taiden here:

Email: millytaiden@gmail.com

Website: http://www.millytaiden.com

Facebook:
http://www.facebook.com/millytaidenpage

Twitter: https://www.twitter.com/millytaiden

If you liked this story, you might also enjoy the following by Milly Taiden:

Sassy Ever After Series

Scent of a Mate *Book One*

A Mate's Bite *Book Two*

Unexpectedly Mated *Book Three*

A Sassy Wedding *Short 3.7*

The Mate Challenge *Book Four*

Sassy in Diapers *Short 4.3*

Fighting for Her Mate *Book Five*

A Fang in the Sass *Book 6*

Also check out the Sassy Ever After Kindle World on Amazon

Shifters Undercover

Bearly in Control *Book One*

Federal Paranormal Unit

Wolf Protector *Federal Paranormal Unit Book One*

Dangerous Protector *Federal Paranormal Unit Book Two*

Unwanted Protector *Federal Paranormal Unit Book Three*

Black Meadow Pack

Sharp Change *Black Meadows Pack Book One*

Caged Heat *Black Meadows Pack Book Two*

Paranormal Dating Agency

Twice the Growl *Book One*

Geek Bearing Gifts *Book Two*

The Purrfect Match *Book Three*

Curves 'Em Right *Book Four*

Tall, Dark and Panther *Book Five*

The Alion King *Book Six*

There's Snow Escape *Book Seven*

Scaling Her Dragon *Book Eight*

In the Roar *Book Nine*

Scrooge Me Hard *Short One*

Bearfoot and Pregnant *Book Ten*

All Kitten Aside *Book Eleven*

Book 12 *(Coming Soon)*

Raging Falls

Miss Taken *Book One*

Miss Matched *Book Two*

Miss Behaved *Book Three (Coming Soon)*

FUR-ocious Lust - Bears

Fur-Bidden *Book One*

Fur-Gotten *Book Two*

Fur-Given Book *Three*

FUR-ocious Lust - Tigers

Stripe-Tease *Book Four*

Stripe-Search *Book Five*

Stripe-Club *Book Six*

Other Works

Wolf Fever

Fate's Wish

Wynter's Captive

Sinfully Naughty Vol. 1

Don't Drink and Hex

Hex Gone Wild

Hex and Kisses

Alpha Owned

Bitten by Night

Seduced by Days

Mated by Night

Taken by Night

Match Made in Hell

Alpha Geek

Contemporary Works

Lucky Chase

Their Second Chance

Club Duo Boxed Set

A Hero's Pride

A Hero Scarred

Wounded Soldiers Set

If you enjoyed the book, please consider leaving a review, even if it's only a line or two; it would make all the difference and would be very much appreciated.

Thank you!

Made in the USA
Middletown, DE
05 January 2017